TANSY

Margaret Trist was born in Dalby, Queensland in 1914. She wrote two story collections, *In the Sun* (1943) and *What Else is There* (1946), plus three novels, *Now That We're Laughing* (1945), *Daddy* (1947) and *Morning in Queensland* (1958) (retitled *Tansy* for this edition). Her work has been praised for its humour, precise characterisation and dialogue, and insight into small town life. Margaret Trist died in 1986.

£1-80

TANSY
MARGARET TRIST

University of Queensland Press

Published 1991 by University of Queensland Press
Box 42, St Lucia, Queensland 4067 Australia

Typeset by University of Queensland Press
Printed in Australia by The Book Printer, Melbourne

Distributed in the USA and Canada by
International Specialized Book Services, Inc.,
5602 N.E. Hassalo Street, Portland, Oregon 97213-3640

Cataloguing in Publication Data
National Library of Australia

Trist, Margaret, 1914-1986.
 [Morning in Queensland]. Tansy.

 I. Title. II. Title: Tansy. (Series : UQP fiction).

A823.3

ISBN 0 7022 2363 8.

to
Dexter and Naelo

1 "All true-born Queenslanders," said Grandfather, "scattered to the four corners of the State; but they didn't cross the MacIntyre."

Tansy screwed up her eyes against the last rays of the sun. She had been watching it, a red ball in the west, hoping to see it drop out of sight. Instead she saw the State of Queensland as an oblong purple box with these unknown aunts and uncles in the gold-splashed corners. At the bottom of the box ran the MacIntyre River dividing it from the next box which was New South Wales. This wasn't accurate, as the MacIntyre formed only a portion of the border, but she was to be indebted to Grandfather all her schooldays for a weakness in geography.

The MacIntyre didn't impress her. Rivers didn't. The only one she had seen was the Condamine and it had had no water in it since she was born. The creek which ran through the town was different. When it rained it had water in it and everyone went to see it. And sure as it had water in it someone was drowned. "You must keep away from the creek, Tansy," her mother always said. "It's treacherous. People take it too lightly."

"I won't cross the MacIntyre," she said now, and had a vision of herself walking down one side of a gully and up the other into the unknown state of New South Wales. Somehow the idea was tempting.

"Should think not," said Grandfather scornfully. "You're a Queenslander too."

"Born on the Darling Downs," she said.

"Oh, the Downs don't matter much," muttered Grandfather. "Just a small bit of Queensland. Wouldn't have picked on the Downs meself. I figure it was a queer set of people who settled in a place without proper burning wood."

Only circumstances had thrust Grandfather onto the Downs. It was the Trenworths, Tansy's mother's people, who had settled here.

"Stringy-bark gum don't burn. It smoulders. Box-tree is better, what there is of it," he said grudgingly.

1

"It was for the sheep," said Tansy.

"Poor dumb critters," said Grandfather. "Even a sheep, if it could talk, would like a shade tree. Wheat, I'd grow, if I had a parcel of land here. Wheat country. You'll see it waving over your head before you're a woman grown. Someone will come who knows."

Tansy remained silent. This was sheep country. She had heard her mother quote her Grand-dad Trenworth as saying so.

"Not," Grandfather admitted, "that I ever stopped long enough anywhere to grow anything."

They were sitting on the back steps watching the sun go down and smoke rising from the chimneys of the houses beyond their own.

Once those houses had not been there, nor had their own. Tansy found it hard to believe. No town at all, no shops, no church, no park, no bridge over the creek. Only the creek and the flat land with its waving yellow grass. A tree here, a tree there, as if by accident. Flat and lonely. The sun coming up in the morning and going down at night with no one to watch it.

Then men driving their sheep before them had crossed the low line of hills far to the east and everything had changed.

"Strathlea, that was my place," went on Grandfather. "Strathallan of Strathlea, that was me."

Her mother had told her that her grandfather's name was Thomas Humphreys Strathallan. Most people, however, called him Black One-Eyed-Tom. She preferred Black One-Eyed-Tom to Thomas Humphreys. But she liked Strathallan of Strathlea best of all. She murmured it to herself.

"A good property, Strathlea. Horses. The finest stud in Queensland in its day, but it dwindled with the years. The racing game is hard. A good place for a stud but a long way from the tracks. A racing man has to be on the track."

The stairs where they were sitting ran down from the back verandah. The kitchen window opened onto the verandah. Now the lamp was lit and saucepan lids clattered warningly. As

2

her mother was quick and deft in her movements, a banging of saucepan lids was on purpose, Tansy knew.

"Dad," her mother's voice came through the window, "do you have to tell her all that again?"

Grandfather moved his game leg to a better position. His white beard quivered as he shouted "Why, what's the matter with it?"

"Didn't we agree that bygones were bygones?"

"You might have."

"I'm thankful she's not old enough to take anything in. And don't shout. You can be heard a mile away."

"If you don't think I'm the right company for her I'll take my two blankets and go. And my horseshoes. Go as I came."

"Don't be silly. No one wants you to go."

He lowered his voice, which still made it louder than other voices. "Mebbe no," he said, "but it sounds like it at times." He fixed his one good eye on Tansy. It was greyish-green in colour and could look fierce under its white, over-hanging brow. "Do I ever tell you anything you oughtn't to hear?"

"No," she said.

He shifted his bulk on the step. "I've a right to be here, haven't I? It was to her I turned when I had nowhere else to go. When I had no more money and couldn't work because my leg went bust and I lost my things, when the Royal Hotel went up. Remember the day I came?"

"No, Grandfather."

"Don't suppose you do. In the go-cart you was then. I had my horseshoes in the tin box, which got blackened by the fire, and my stick which I made myself from a piece of blackwood off Strathlea, and my two blankets rolled in a swag on my back. New, them blankets. Swapped a bottle of rum with the Blacks for them. Blacks get them free. Whenever you see them blankets with the pink, blue and green squares, you know what they are. Government issue to the Blacks. That's all I had and no money. Could have sold the horseshoes, I daresay. The best collection in Australia. Two hundred and fifty-one of them. All from my favourite horses, didn't just take them from any old horse. So I wouldn't part with them. I was in straits and I turned to her. Rightly so; my eldest son's wife, ain't she? The right to take me in is hers. I didn't pass her by and go to one of me own daughters, did I?"

"No."

"And I make no complaints that Jarge is rarely here, do I?"

"George is up North," Tansy said.

The old man lowered his voice. "Likely to remain there too. Not good for a man to be tied to a woman's petticoats. She'd get on all right with Jarge if she only would allow his ways are different from hers. She married him, didn't she? As he was. And started right in to change him into a Trenworth. Jarge is as like a Trenworth as chalk is like cheese."

Tansy remained politely silent. Her mother had been "Meredith Trenworth, that beautiful girl with the world at her feet", before she ran off with George.

"Oh, I daresay there's some good in Trenworths," said Grandfather hastily, remembering that his granddaughter belonged to the Trenworths too. "But set, awful set, in their habits. You could see it in her —" he jerked his thumb over his shoulder towards the kitchen — "when she first came to Strathlea. Eloped with Jarge, you know, rode sidesaddle from the Condamine to the MacIntyre. A bit of a way when you come to look at it. And a bad beginning when they got there, from her point of view, but could have been overlooked. It was a pity it was Em went out to hold the bridle for her to dismount. But Em was like that, always rushing to do things. Em was hard to gainsay. The spit of him."

Tansy looked at him inquiringly. She knew the names of the aunts and uncles who were now gathered in the corners of that oblong box which was Queensland, but she had not heard of Em before.

"Is Em another aunty?" Tansy asked. Though already over-endowed with relations she could always spare affection for another one.

4

"Not an aunty. More a — well, a cousin will do. But what it all boils down to is that *she* don't go the right way about handling Jarge. Not biddable enough, she ain't. Jarge is well enough in his way."

"Yes," said Tansy, though she didn't have a good opinion of George, who had turned up several times and disrupted life badly. Now and again her mother went up North to see George, leaving her with Aunt Jessie.

"A fly-by-night is Jarge," said Grandfather. "It's useless of anyone to expect him to stop anywhere. I was the same in my younger days, but I didn't get married, till later on. Then I married Annie, the plainest girl north of the MacIntyre. You could leave her to mind the place knowing no one would bother her none. But she wasn't any great shakes at minding the place. Always toting childer about or digging up the garden, while the fences rotted. And never thinking to remember which day the foal was dropped! Makes a difference, that does. You get home and it's a great horse, it's not as easy as all that to tell how old it is. But now she's gone I'd be the last to say a word against her. She shouldn't have done that. I had a good thirty year start on her and took it for natural she'd be tending me when my strength was gone.

"Poor Anne-Margaret," Tansy said sympathetically.

"She was always weak, my Annie," said Grandfather. "And the place going off like that over her head, finished things. She couldn't understand what it was all about. Oh well, I did my best to save it. There wasn't a deader certainty foaled than that horse, and, things being as they were, it was all or nothing."

"Dad! What are you telling her now?"

"I was saying," Grandfather called loudly, "that the sun's gone and it's high time we brought in the wood."

Strathallan, once of Strathlea, that property of which he spoke so often and so lovingly, where he had lingered seldom, and which had passed from him when he put it on a racehorse one spring meeting in Brisbane, marched towards the woodheap with as much dignity as his game leg and walking stick allowed. He was a large, lumbering old man who, in this year of our Lord, 1919, was enjoying his ninety-second year. Hale and hearty, memory undimmed, energetic by day, a sound sleeper by night, partial to his food, interested in anyone and everyone who had ever been born, anything and everything that happened, he found the world a satisfactory place. His granddaughter, Tansy Strathallan, born and being bred, if that is what her mother's and her grandfather's efforts on her behalf could be called, in Goombudgerie, North West Darling Downs, walked beside him.

The sun had gone, but fingers of light spread fanwise in the western sky. Small, fleecy, purple clouds glowed saffron at the edges. A black bird flew high overhead. They looked up to watch it, standing silhouetted against the woodstack in the last light of day. Then the quick dusk gathered. It came so swiftly. Indigo shadows flung over the land, the first twinkling of stars in the darkening sky.

"The dark'll catch us if we're not quick," said Grandfather. He began throwing the chopped wood into a handcart. Tansy stooped and gathered chips into an old tin dish. They went in with a ringing sound which made her laugh.

In the kitchen Meredith Strathallan laid the table for supper. "Of course she doesn't take anything in," she said aloud. A small woman just past her twenty-sixth birthday, her dark hair was piled on top of her head, tendrils escaping on her forehead and at the nape of her neck. Her eyes were green and her skin olive, her mouth a firmly held cerise line. She held it like that to subdue it. The beauty of her girlhood was with her still but overlaid by a surprised and anxious look and lines were already etched beside her mouth and between her brows. "And what could a child of that age make of it all, anyway?" She clasped her hands in front of her and sighed.

The sigh was her admission to herself that she had gone North once too often.

The Strathallan homestead on Strathlea had had twenty-three rooms, but the Strathallan residence in Palm-grove Street, Goombudgerie, had only four rooms of equal size, with a verandah back and front. Two were bedrooms, one behind the other on the left-hand side. The front room on the right-hand side was the living-room and the room behind it the kitchen. The left-hand portion of the back verandah had been enclosed at one time to make a bathroom and was referred to as such, though it held a single bed and lumber and the Strathallans took their baths in the kitchen. The rooms were sparely furnished, necessary articles of varnished pine taking up very little space. Only the kitchen floor was covered with linoleum. The cypress pine floorboards of the other rooms had been darkened with Condy's crystals and were polished once in a while. Most of the year the doors and windows were wide open, day and night. Only during a summer storm, or the few weeks in August when the westerly winds blew, were they closed. There was plenty of fresh air and sunlight and a clean smell, mingled at times with smoke from the wood stove.

As Meredith said, it was a roof over their heads, and for this she was thankful. It was owned by her parents; she had the use of it for as long as she might need it.

She liked to feel independent but did not feel so when she entered the kitchen next morning. Having admitted one fact, she had had to follow it up during a sleepless night with the admission that the situation would have to be faced. With Meredith, "facing situations" mostly had something to do with money.

The old man was there before her, busy cracking pinewood across his knee. His cheeks were pink above his white beard, his one eye glanced at her alertly, bright and fierce under its overhanging brow.

"Dad," she said, "there's something I want to talk to you about. I'm afraid we're in straits."

"Again!" he demanded. "What now? Paid the rates, didn't

we? That bit of wood I cut for Tompkins and the rags you're always stitching at! Thought it fixed it up?"

"Oh, yes; the rates are paid."

"Well, has the store bill got away again? If so, that fellow Chaseling is a robber. My bit of tobacco and sugar and flour don't add up to much."

"It's not the store bill either. It's just — since the last time I went North I haven't been as well as I was, and I don't know how long I can keep up my sewing. Jessie says there's an old-age pension you should be getting. If we had something like that we could manage nicely. Would you mind?"

She looked at him, her eyes bright and green as they were when she was anxious. Their glance was keen, though according to herself, their sight was about to fail. "I don't know how I do so much sewing, with my eyes," she often said. She had on her red kimono with the white storks embroidered upon it; her hair lay against her shoulders in dark, tendrily plaits.

The old man snapped another piece of pine across his knee and put it with the kindling in the stove. "Mind what? Is it money? Can't say I've ever had any objection to money."

"But this is from the government, and I didn't know if you'd like taking money from the government."

"Why not? I'll take it from anywhere I can get it. Reckon they owe me something anyway. I never could figure why they gave blankets to the Blacks and me nothing."

"We're not talking about Blacks. We must talk about this."

"It's a poor conversation that can't take in this and that on the way," he grumbled. "How much do I get?"

"I don't know. We have to go into the matter, and I can't go into it without you."

"Should think not. You could make a start by asking your folks. They'd know."

"They mightn't like the idea. It comes out of the taxpayers' money, I suppose, and they might feel they were supporting you in an indirect fashion."

Not the least of Meredith's troubles was her family's attitude to the old man. She was sensitive about it, if the old man wasn't. Then there was his attitude to them which she was also sensitive about, though they weren't. She had, however, one comfort. She was doing her duty. She had her own ideas about these things. Circumstances didn't alter them.

"Why shouldn't they?" he asked now. "They've got plenty, and all through stopping in one place. Not the way to live. The Blacks have the right idea. Eat one place out and go somewhere else."

Meredith ignored the subject of the Blacks. "They've given us this house to live in and that's a lot. I don't know how we'd get on if we were paying rent." She sank into the old wicker chair by the stove.

He looked at her sitting in his chair winding one of her plaits over her fingers. Meredith was able to do only one thing at a time. When she talked, she talked; the fact that breakfast was getting behind was of no importance to her. It was most important to him.

"Come to think of it, Jarge should give you some. Ask him for it, Meredith."

"I'm past asking George for anything he doesn't give of his own free will and accord." She sighed and wound the plait over her fingers faster. "I wonder what he thinks we live on?" she cried angrily.

"He knows you've got a fist with the needle," the old man said placatingly. He didn't want her to entirely overlook the breakfast. He wasn't much at cooking: "You having two rashers or three?"

"I'm not having any."

"I'll have five then. The little crittur don't have more than one."

Meredith watched the rest of the week's supply of bacon go into the pan. "That's what happens to the store bill."

"What's that?"

"Nothing." If an old man's pleasure in the last years of his life was eating, she wasn't the one to stop him.

9

"He never thinks of sending money," she said resentfully.

"But he sends bits of joolry. Never saw such a one for bits of joolry as Jarge."

"I wonder where he thinks I go, to wear them," said Meredith. "The last brooch he sent was from India."

"What's he doing in India?"

"He took some horses from Darwin to Bombay."

"You didn't tell me that!" The old man placed the kettle on the blaze and pushed in the damper. His one eye had a faraway look. "Never thought of that part of the racing game before. Can't say I blame Jarge for being in on it. I'd like to try it for meself. Fine thing, taking a sea trip with horses. Has he told you of it in his letter? He writes a good letter, does Jarge."

Meredith remained silent. It was those pleasant charming letters which had drawn her North so often. On paper George was an amiable, entertaining, desirable person. Off it, he was a long, stringy man, fifteen years older than herself, with no idea of his duty as a husband and a father.

"It sounds something I could do. There's no better judge of horseflesh in this State than me!"

"Don't be silly," said Meredith. "What about your leg? You can't get to the front gate without your stick, and you can't get down town unless Holy Joe takes you."

"A pity," he admitted. "But mebbe it's for the best. The government mightn't give me this other money if I went to India. We better set about the pension quick, Meredith."

"Yes," agreed Meredith, "but we won't talk about it further at the moment. Tansy's coming."

Tansy came in carefully, her face shining with importance. She was carrying the billy-can Grandfather had made from a large treacle tin, brimming with milk. She wasn't spilling a drop. "The Hogan boy brought it. I gave him the threepence."

Too much talk and too little breakfast had frayed Grandfather's temper. "Thruppence," he roared. "Thruppence just for milk, which comes natural and free. Milk shouldn't be charged for. That's where the money goes, Meredith. Fine sort of people who bring milk and charge for it.''

Meredith and Tansy looked at him anxiously. The Hogans were a block away; but as they sometimes heard Mr Hogan telling Mrs Hogan what he thought of her, they were afraid Mr Hogan might hear Grandfather's opinion of him.

"Mr Hogan does it as a favour," said Meredith. "We get more from him than we would from the dairy for the same price. Milk is charged for in a town because the food for the cows has to be bought. Things have changed since your day.''

"Seems so," he muttered. "And for the worse!''

2 A little later on Meredith and Grandfather went to Brisbane to interview the Member of Parliament for the District about the pension, and Tansy went again to Aunt Jessie.

Aunt Jessie lived on the outskirts of Goombudgerie. Her chimney was the farthest one Tansy and Grandfather could see when they sat on the back steps in the late afternoon, and it puffed smoke more vigorously and in a neater fashion than any other chimney. The house was similar to Tansy's own, only Aunt Jessie was a natural born housekeeper and Meredith wasn't. Things shone in Aunt Jessie's house. Also Aunt Jessie had green fingers and Meredith did not. Besides, Aunt Jessie had Uncle Joe, who amused himself putting a lick of paint on the house every so often. They only had Grandfather who had never put a lick of paint on anything in his life. So their house was unpainted and weathered grey, while Aunt Jessie's was bright pink, the window sashes and door frames picked out in maroon. Despite all this Tansy preferred her own house.

Tansy had called Jessie and Joe Sprockett "aunt" and "uncle" from babyhood. In point of fact Aunt Jessie thought it forward of Meredith to call her "Jessie". But she forebore to say so. Which showed how much she thought of the whole

Trenworth family. There was no one else on earth to whom she forebore to say anything.

"Don't tell me Meredith's gone North," said Uncle Joe when he saw Tansy. He was a tall, thin man, with kindly brown eyes and a long, drooping moustache.

"No," replied Aunt Jessie, "she's gone with Black One-Eyed-Tom to see about the pension. If you ask me I don't think she'll go North again. That George has just about worn himself out in her estimation."

Aunt Jessie was thinner than Uncle Joe and didn't reach to his shoulder when she stood beside him. Her hair was dark, pulled tightly back from her face into a neat bun at the back. Her skin shone from soap and water and her blue eyes peered through steel-reemed spectacles. She put an overall over Tansy's dress and tied the tapes firmly.

"About time," said Uncle Joe. "I could never make head nor tail of it. Where she met the fellow —"

"She met him under the Sawpit Tree," said Tansy.

"Little girls should be seen and not heard," said Aunt Jessie.

"And what she saw in him —" continued Uncle Joe.

"He sings beautifully," put in Tansy quickly. While she didn't care for George herself, she felt the need to defend him on Meredith's behalf.

"What?" demanded Aunt Jessie.

"Mother can't listen to John McCormick now," Tansy explained. "It makes her feel as if George is in the very room. He sings George's songs."

"Did you hear that?" Aunt Jessie looked incredulously at Uncle Joe.

Uncle Joe looked at Tansy. "Born that time of the heatwave just after the Great War started.

"I was five the last time the amaryllis came out," said Tansy.

"Oh, were you? Well, act like five and not as a baby," said Aunt Jessie. "Run outside and pick the weeds from the lettuce bed. Don't start playing around and forget about it. A big girl should work. Work is what we are put in this world to do and I'm not sorry, when I think of the mischief some would get into without it. And don't get dirty. If you do, saying you couldn't help it won't be of use. I know better.''

As Tansy went Aunt Jessie's voice came after her. "Meredith says she doesn't take anything in. What would you say she's doing, Joe?''

"Little pigs have ears that flap,'' returned Uncle Joe cheerfully.

Tansy was fond of Uncle Joe. She was also fond of little pigs. But she didn't care about being called one by him.

The lettuce bed was well built up, which gave it a fat, bursting look. Like all good Darling Downs earth it was rich and black, and the plump, tight lettuces shone pale green against it. In each lettuce, drops of moisture from a recent watering sparkled like the stones in the earrings and brooches George sent Meredith. The soil was damp, too. She dug her fingers in this her native earth and went on digging while her mind wandered to far-off Brisbane where Meredith and Grandfather were seeing the Member for the District.

"What do you think you are, child? A mole?'' Aunt Jessie demanded half an hour later. "Joe, Joe, come and see what she's done now!''

They were away only a few days and returned home pleased. The Member had been courteous and sent them to someone, who sent them to someone else, who told them they could obtain the forms to be filled in at the post office in Goombudgerie.

Thomas Humphreys Strathallan began filling them in, taking care with his writing. "The pity is that I'm away to a late start. Could have been getting this for years.''

"Where were you born?'' asked Meredith.

"Under a bullock dray.''

"Yes; but where was the bullock dray?''

13

"North of the MacIntyre."

"Oh, dear!" she said, "I wonder if they'll take that. Have you a birth certificate?"

"Not that I know of."

"Dad, if you are ninety-two now, you must have been born in 1827. Could you have been born north of the MacIntyre then?"

"Why not?"

"Queensland as a State wasn't founded."

"I don't care if it was founded or not. You're not trying to tell me I'm a New South Welshman, are you?"

"I feel you might be," said Meredith cautiously.

"Well, I'm not," the old man said decidedly.

"We may have to go into this much more fully. Leave that and fill in the space after religion. You put Roman Catholic there."

"Why?"

"Because you are one. The priest comes to see you every month."

"Your idea, not mine. I've never had anything to do with any of it."

"Anne-Margaret was a Catholic and all your children are."

"Which doesn't make me one. My mother was a Methody."

"Were you born and christened that?" Meredith's eyes grew big and dark green with surprise.

"'Spect so! Born anyway. Can't say for sure I was christened."

"But why ever didn't you tell me?"

"Never thought. You didn't ask."

"How can I face the priest when he hears this?"

"It'll get rid of him for sure," said the old man gleefully. "And don't think of putting the other one in his place. I might be out. With this money I'll be able to get around more."

It was several months before the pension was granted. However, the day came when Grandfather set off in Holy Joe's cab

14

to collect his first money. When he returned he had not only funds for the next fortnight but a small fortune in the way of back money as THEY had been kindly saving it up since the date of the first application.

The pension, while a blessing, was not an unmitigated one, as Meredith said. She arranged for Holy Joe to call for the old man every second Thursday and gave instructions for them to go to the post office, collect the pension and return home immediately. Holy Joe and his cab had appeared in Goombudgerie along with the railway and, according to himself, he intended to see the railway out. He was a sad looking little man who had once suffered tragedy in the form of the only likely looking girl he had known jilting him. His name came from the way he said his prayers louder than the priest in church. He believed prayers should be said loudly so the Almighty would get the gist of them. Holy Joe had a poor sense of time and it turned out that he shared one of Grandfather's weaknesses. Meredith had to take to making the fortnightly trip with them; even so, they sometimes gave her the slip.

In this manner her father-in-law acquired friends. In a very short space of time a number of old men were to be found gathered of an afternoon on her back verandah. They knocked the ashes of their tobacco into her potted fishbone ferns and spoke of the days that were over and gone forever.

Tansy was allowed to sit with Grandfather and his friends and heard tales of cattle-duffing, horse-stealing and sheep-rustling. She soon knew all about changing the brands and what colour dye would overcome grey dapplings on a pony. She was interested in two-up, shaking the dice, taking plunges, and when to lay bets and when not.

As Meredith had been a Trenworth before her marriage, so her mother had been a Cuthbertson. The first Trenworth family had been with Jeremy Grant Whittaker, one of the early men to come across the low line of hills to take up land. J.G. Whittaker had called his station Derrick Plains.

The Cuthbertsons had come later, but both Tansy's Great-grandfather Cuthbertson and Great-grandfather Trenworth had been shepherds on Derrick Plains. As Grandfather Strathallan liked to talk of Strathlea, so Meredith liked to talk of Derrick Plains. She had not been born there but on the Trenworth property, Land's End. By the time of Meredith's birth Derrick Plains as a station was no more. As the property of Woodlands had become the town of Goombudgerie, that of Derrick Plains had become a township.

Tansy knew that Derrick Plains was "out there"; that is, far out beyond Aunt Jessie's neatly puffing chimney. Land's End was "out there" somewhere too. And in the same direction was the small property by the river where her great-grandparents, the Cuthbertsons, had lived up till this time.

However, shortly after the granting of the pension the Cuthbertsons came into Goombudgerie to live. They settled in what was known as the Big House round Hogan's corner and Tansy was delighted to have relations so close. The pension, the pink-and-white lolly stick Grandfather Strathallan brought her every second Thursday, the frequent calls of Holy Joe, and Cuthie and Pap Cuthbertson (as they were known to their grandchildren, and now to Tansy, their great-grandchild) coming into town, were closely associated in her mind. Pap was ill, so Meredith would go to see them, leaving Tansy to sit on the verandah with Grandfather and his friends.

Tansy and Cuthie were not particularly impressed with one another at their first meeting. Cuthie, who was seventy-two and had had "looks" all her life, liked her descendants to have them also. She did not care for snub noses, over-big mouths and eyes, skins that freckled, and hair that tangled on its owner's head instead of brushing into smooth curls. This sort of thing was bred in the bone, she considered, and didn't hesitate to say so. Cuthie herself had a fine, fair skin, china blue eyes and ropes of silver hair swathed about her head. She was tall, with what she called "good proportion". Though Mere-

16

dith stuck to her opinion that Tansy was average size for her age, Cuthie implied that Tansy was either underfed or ailing.

As Tansy had always been satisfied with herself and approved by Meredith and Grandfather and even Aunt Jessie, she was unpleasantly surprised at this sort of attitude in her own great-grandmother.

Before Cuthie made her departure she said, "What faith did you have her baptised in, Meredith?"

Meredith had to admit that Tansy had not been baptised at all. She considered men should have the say in these matters and, as George was of a different persuasion from herself, had waited all these years for his ruling on the matter.

"What nonsense!" said Cuthie. "Consider me, not George. I don't want it bruited about that a great-grandchild of mine is unchristened."

So Meredith, who, as even Tansy could see, was liable to fret about the most unlikely subjects at this time, worried aloud over it for several weeks.

Grandfather, to help things along, recited verses about a boy who ran into a hollow log rather than be baptised. "Come out and be christened, you divil," he would shout in high glee as they sat on the back steps.

Meredith sometimes forgot things, so Tansy hoped she would forget this. But in the middle of a weekday morning Meredith put on the black-and-white check costume which had been her best as long as Tansy remembered, and the sailor hat with the black spotted veil through which her eyes looked greener than ever, and took Tansy off to the rectory.

The Rector, after pointing out that it was more usual to be christened after matins while the congregation was still gathered, left the preparation of his sermon, collected his wife, housekeeper and verger as godparents, and they went to the church.

While everything was being made ready, Tansy took fright and ran away.

She made a headlong dash, the Rector followed behind with

his robes flying, Meredith behind the Rector, the long tight skirt of the check costume impeding her progress, the veil on her hat fluttering, crying, "Not on the road, Tansy, not on the road."

The Rector also had long skirts but they were wide and full and, apparently used to chasing escaping members of his flock, he caught up with Tansy quickly. He grasped both her hands in one of his and pulled her after him back to the church.

"Now what are we going to call her?" he cried at Meredith above Tansy's screams.

"Why, Tansy," shouted Meredith.

"Tansy. But what is Tansy short for?"

"Sheila. I meant to call her Sheila. Tansy came about."

"Ah!" exclaimed the Rector loudly.

"No, no," cried Meredith. "You'll have to make it Tansy; she's used to it."

"Tansy Sheila, then," cried the Rector.

Hastily and wetly Tansy was christened. On the way home her tears fell all over the card printed in blue and red and scrolls of gold that recorded the fact that she was now a member of the Church of England.

"I was never so ashamed in my life," said Meredith when they were home again and Tansy sat hiccoughing on Grandfather's knee as he restored her with weak tea well laced with milk and sugar. "But it's over and done with and quite off my mind. I'll let sleeping dogs lie if George comes any time. I feel everything's in order now. I can take this last month in peace and quiet."

"If I know you, Meredith," said Grandfather, "you're bound to find something to fret over."

3 "What is it now, Dolores?" asked Meredith.
"Mum says I may take Tansy for a walk this afternoon, Mrs Strathallan."

"Does she? Well, I don't know," Meredith sighed. Dolores came over every afternoon to ask to take Tansy for a walk, and about every eighth or ninth afternoon Meredith, worn out by what she called "that child's persistence", let Tansy go. "Very well. As it happens I'm trying to make a sponge and she wants to lick the bowl before I even have the ingredients in it."

"Oh, isn't she funny?" said Dolores, feeling to see if her hair ribbon was in place. Dolores' hair was in process of growing. It hung to her shoulders in straight brown wisps and was gathered back from her forehead in a meagre plait, hairpinned to her head and surmounted by the bow. Her face was long and white, her nose sharp. She had two very new, very white teeth, showing under her narrow top lip, and her eyes were a light inquisitive blue.

"Just take her a little way," said Meredith. "To the old convent and back."

"All right, Mrs Strathallan, I'll do that." And Dolores took Tansy's hand.

Dolores, two years older than Tansy, lived across the road. She had a younger brother, Dalzell, and there were three children older than she was. Mrs Rowlands was a member of the Mothers' Union, sang in the church choir and took interest in her neighbours in a Christian manner.

Meredith had no time for what she called strangers, by which she meant people who had come after the springing up of the town, when the days of the big properties were over. She found the little company she needed among her own family and the few still remaining who had sprung "direct from Derrick Plains", as she put it. So, while she could be friendly with Jessie and Joe Sprockett, who had been under-nursemaid and blacksmith on Derrick Plains in the last days of its glory; and thaw immediately to the man who brought the wood because his uncle had been woodsman "out there", and have a happy easy acquaintance with Doctor John and his wife because Doctor John's father had come direct from Old England to be a jackaroo on the Plains, she turned a cold front to any of the "strangers" who tried to befriend her. Mrs Rowlands was unaware of being a "stranger". She was willing to make allowances for Mrs Strathallan owing to the position in which she was placed and persisted in good deeds. Meredith said "botheration" every time Mrs Rowlands' neighbourly duty was directed at herself.

The Old Convent was farther along the street and consisted of some charred stumps, crumpled tanks and prickly bushes on which grew red berries. Meredith usually stood outside the gate with her hand shading her eyes and watched Tansy and Dolores to and fro. But this afternoon, owing to the sponge, she remained in the kitchen.

When they were outside the gate Dolores said, "I'm tired of going to the old convent and back. It's nothing to look at. Just burnt down, that's all. The new convent is better."

"Yes," said Tansy.

"But it's across the creek. We couldn't go across the creek, could we?"

"No," said Tansy.

"I'll tell you what, we'll go to the park. The park isn't across the creek," said Dolores virtuously. She gave a backward glance at the Strathallan house, hurried Tansy across the road and round the corner. She dropped Tansy's hand, went back to the corner and peeped round the fence. "We haven't been seen," she announced. She took Tansy's hand again and they proceeded in leisurely fashion.

She pointed across the road. "The pub," she said; "my father doesn't go there, does yours? Oh, of course, you haven't got one. How silly of me. Mum says I'm not to mention it."

"No," said Tansy. "We've got Grandfather." But she was more interested in the pub, which was a long, low building with plants in painted tubs along the verandah. There was a blue glass door with a space above and below and letters on it which broke in two as the door swung when a man came out. Horses were tethered to a rail outside, and a cattle dog with its tongue lolling lay in the dust of the footpath.

"You'd be sorry if he went there. No money for food then!"

"Our food is brought in."

"What do you mean?"

"Granny and Grand-dad Trenworth live in the country, so when anyone's coming in they send things in to us."

"Oh! You are funny people! Don't you go to Chaselings?"

"Yes."

"Well, what do you get?"

"Treacle-syrup and matching cotton and pen-nibs."

"That's what you wouldn't be able to buy if your father went to the pub."

"Mr Chaseling gives them to us. And a bag of lollies, too."

"Well, I never! Oh, but you are a baby! They're not given to you, they're charged. You get the lollies when you pay."

Instead of crossing the bridge they went down the steps at the side. "Don't look back," said Dolores "there might be a swaggie. If they grab you you're never seen again."

Tansy did look back and there was a swagman leaning over a fire with a blackened billy-can above it. He looked like one of Grandfather's friends and she wasn't frightened of him.

They went through the park gate. Inside the park there were five willows on one side of the path, on the other a patch of kurrajong trees. Meredith had told Tansy that on the site of the park the homestead of Woodlands had once stood, and that Woodlands had taken its name from this patch of trees. The willows had been planted by the Governor's Lady when she came to pay a visit. The kurrajongs had been there always, the patch of green almost all there was to be seen on that wide plain when the first white men came. Tansy conveyed what she could of this to Dolores wasn't very interested.

"Mum says you should learn to talk for yourself, instead of repeating what your elders say," said Dolores. "Mum says it's a great pity about you."

"What is?"

"Oh, everything," said Dolores. "Now just look at that." Amongst the kurrajongs was a seat on which a man and

21

woman sat side by side. "Tut! Tut!" went Dolores. "The Mothers' Union is going to have that seat removed."

"Why?"

"Look what happens. People sit on it."

Out of the wood they came to a little round building with a pointed roof and no walls but a railing. They went up steps one side, crossed the board floor, climbed on the railing, jumped down and then down the steps on the other side.

"Did you like our Rotunda?" asked Dolores, but before Tansy could say, "Yes, I did," veered off the path and pointed to two small, galvanized iron buildings, side by side. "Never go near there!"

"Why?"

"They have S-H-I-T written on the walls."

"I can't spell. Say it."

"No! No, I couldn't. I couldn't say that."

"S-H-I-T," Tansy said wonderingly.

"Don't! Don't! It's dreadful." Dolores hurried her off to the other end of the park.

Here there was a large three-barred gate. "That's to come off and Our Ornamental Gates will be there. And over there will be the Memorial to Our Glorious Dead. We haven't any, have you?"

"Yes. But some of them aren't buried. It was the flood."

"The war, silly, the Great War. It's a pity we won't be on, but Dad couldn't get to the front; his duty lay here."

They were now wandering towards the creek and the big old gum whose exposed roots went down into the water. The late afternoon was hushed, carts rumbling over the bridge, the clippety-clop of horses sounding far away. The last sunlight fell on the park in a steady glow, while the buildings across the creek were shadowed. Tansy's eyes were fixed on the narrow muddy stream of water flowing so lazily the surface barely stirred.

They stopped by the gum and Dolores pointed across the creek. "That building's for the Electric Light Plant, which won't be any use, Dad says. It's being bought secondhand from Bundaberg where it's given nothing but trouble. We'll be paying for what we're not getting."

Dead gum leaves lay in little heaps under the tree. Tansy disturbed a heap with the toe of her sandal. Then she let go Dolores' hand and stepped out onto one of the roots of the tree. The next moment she was above her knees in water.

"Oh!" said Dolores. "Why ever did you go and do that?" She hauled her out, took off her wet sandals and began wiping them diligently on the grass. "You could have been drowned! And what would your mother have said then? I'd have caught it and it wouldn't have been fair. You did it all yourself, you did, didn't you? I didn't push you or anything." With her own hanky she wiped Tansy's legs. "Now you don't look as if you've been in the creek. You haven't, have you? What are you going to say when you get home?"

"That I didn't fall in the creek."

"No, no. You don't say anything. And you haven't been to the park either. You've been to the old convent. Promise."

Tansy promised.

"Spit your death."

Tansy did that, too.

When she arrived home Meredith was over seeing Pap, and Grandfather was out chopping wood in the dusk. The fire was blazing in the stove the way Grandfather liked it. Tansy took off her sandals, opened the oven door and popped them inside, well to the back.

Meredith returned in time for tea. She was preoccupied and hardly glanced at Tansy. During tea she said to Grandfather, "Doctor John can't do any more. It's a question of time. The sooner the better, I would think, but I wouldn't say it to Cuthie. It's hard to see a good man suffer. Did you shiver, Tansy?"

"No, Mother." She had, several times. Meredith's attention soon went elsewhere.

"What wood are you burning in the stove, Dad? There's rather a funny smell."

"That of the load he brought before last," said Grandfather. "He does not always oblige with what I ask, but hardly his fault, the terrain not growing what it should for hot, clean burning. I can't say I have much time for the sort of people who set themselves down in the middle of a treeless plain without proper wood for burning."

Tansy went to bed early but was restless and from time to time shivered violently. However, she didn't call Meredith as she already knew her own habit of saying what she didn't mean to say. Her promise to Dolores weighed more heavily on her than the thought of her sandals cooking in the oven. She couldn't get them out as Grandfather sat in the kitchen till late at night reading the newspapers, of which he had a fine collection, never throwing one away, or allowing Meredith to use one — to cut out a pattern or to wrap up things. From the kitchen at midnight, Grandfather's voice often shouted news of happenings which had taken place several years earlier.

Tansy lay tossing and shivering; guilt of several kinds lay on her soul. She screwed her eyes tightly shut, sleep might have descended, only she heard voices at the front door. Those of Meredith and Mrs Rowlands. Sleep vanished.

"I've come to see if Tansy took any harm from her dip," said Mrs Rowlands.

"What dip?" asked Meredith.

"When she fell in the creek. Dolores rescued her. If Dolores hadn't been there goodness knows what would have happened."

"But what were they doing in the park? Dolores should not have taken Tansy there."

"Tansy would go there, so Dolores had to go, too. Dolores never goes to the park without permission. Then she ran away from Dolores and jumped in the water. Only that Dolores went after her so quickly it might have been an unhappy story. But I haven't come here to censure the child; it's a friendly visit to make sure she's all right.''

"Well, thank you, Mrs Rowlands. It is kind of you. I'll have to speak to her. I didn't know anything about it.''

"You didn't! She is a funny child! Fancy holding it back. Dolores tells me everything.''

As they exchanged goodnights Tansy sat up. From time to time she had been told that she was about to get *what-for*, but it had never happened. She felt it was going to happen now but was so miserable anyway she hardly cared.

Meredith came into the room and turned up the lamp. Her face was stern. "Tansy, how many times have I told you not to go near water?''

She tried to answer but the words strangled in her throat. She felt her chest heave and started to cough, strange, loud coughs like none she had ever had before. Despite the solemnity of the occasion she recognised these coughs as interesting and looked appealingly at Meredith, whose face confirmed her conviction. However distressing, those coughs had come at the right moment. *What-for* was postponed till the future.

"Oh, darling, see what you've done through being so naughty. You've taken whooping-cough from falling in the creek. And at a time like this! Whatever am I going to do?''

"I can't help it, Mother,'' said Tansy as well as she could amongst the coughs; "it won't stop.''

"I'll get you some milk and honey. Better whooping-cough, I suppose, than being drowned as you might well have been.''

"I only fell in a little way.''

"Four inches are enough to drown a child.''

She was given hot milk and petted and Meredith lay on the bed beside her with her arms around her. Which Tansy felt was right. She hadn't wanted to fall in the creek. She tried to go to sleep with her eyes open but failed.

"Mother.''

"Yes, darling.''

"You know that funny smell at tea?''

25

"What about it?"

"I think it was my sandals."

"Why? Where are your sandals?"

"In the back of the oven."

"Good heavens! Why ever didn't you tell me?" Meredith went off to the kitchen and came back. "It's too late to do anything about them now," she said resignedly. "They're ruined. You'll have to stay inside till I can get you another pair."

Tansy was now able to sorrow fully about her sandals. She sorrowed in great gulps and sobs. She knew what a bother sandals were to Meredith, who, owing to people who didn't mind her having what was over when she made a dress, could make Tansy's clothes at little cost. But sandals had to be bought.

"You mustn't go on like that just over sandals," said Meredith. "Please don't worry about sandals. Sandals are not so important in themselves. It's the exigency of living which makes them so. It's all wrong, and as far as you're concerned I don't want a breath of that sort to reach you till you're grownup. Not then, either, I hope."

So it was all right and Tansy patted Meredith and they settled down once more.

"Mother."

"Yes, darling."

"What is S-H-I-T?"

"Oh!" cried Meredith, jumping up, "this is far too much. Where did you hear that?"

"I saw it on a wall," said Tansy.

"You what? That woman can keep that child away from here in future!" She took the lamp, turned it up, and went to the sitting-room with it. Through the open door Tansy saw her at the table writing a letter. She went out their front door, was away several minutes, then returned. "There," she said, "I put it under her door, and that is the end of Mrs Rowlands and Dolores as far as we're concerned."

But it wasn't. In no time Mrs Rowlands was back at their

door. "My Dolores did not teach your child to say S-H-I-T," she said.

"You are not trying to say, I hope, that Tansy taught Dolores S-H-I-T."

"If Dolores has ever heard of S-H-I-T she must have."

"Tansy cannot spell C-A-T, let alone S-H-I-T. Where would she hear it if not from Dolores?"

"Tansy is about all the time with a dubious old man. When my Dalzell came home from here the other day he called our unmentionable a dunny."

"Who's talking of dunnies?" asked Grandfather interestedly from the kitchen.

"I am," said Mrs Rowlands, "and I won't have my children call them that."

"If they ain't a dunny, what are they?" demanded Grandfather, coming to the door.

Meredith, having had words with Grandfather over this matter, was silent.

"I don't care what they are," said Mrs Rowlands, "but when it comes to my children being contaminated —"

"They ain't as bad as all that," said Grandfather. "But I was in a dunny once when it was blowed over by a storm and I can tell you —"

"Dad! Dad! Mrs Rowlands does not want to hear about that."

"I certainly do not," said Mrs Rowlands, "but it's plain for anyone to see where S-H-I-T came from. In future please keep it to yourselves. Goodnight."

"Very uncalled for," said Meredith returning to the bedroom. "Very uncalled for, indeed."

"But Mother, what is it?" asked Tansy. "Just tell me what it is."

"It's a very ugly word and please never use it. Oh, there you go, coughing again!

From the night the whooping-cough started, Aunt Jessie

came down often, and Cuthie left Pap several times to come over.

Tansy whooped often, even after she was up and let out in the sunshine. She whooped until she was exhausted and fell down where she was, which mostly happened to be in a far part of the paddock. Meredith came running to pick her up and carry her back to the house.

"I'm warning you, Meredith," said Cuthie one day, "you'll loosen up and be laid up, before expected."

"But what can I do, Cuthie? I just can't let her die at a time like this!"

"Seems to me it wouldn't hurt her any. She'd know not to, next time."

Tansy was not fond of Cuthie in those days.

* * *

"But I can't sleep there, Aunt Jessie. That's the bathroom. I sleep in with Mother."

"You'll sleep where you're put," said Aunt Jessie, "and don't go bothering your mother; she's sick. In my opinion the blame's at your door, so don't go making things worse than they are. Come along."

"Grandfather, I don't want —"

"Do as you're told for once," said Grandfather. "Can't you see we're at sixes and sevens?"

Tansy, offended, followed Aunt Jessie, who hardly waited till she was in bed before blowing out the candle. "Now cough your head off for all I care," she said by way of goodnight.

Tansy didn't sleep well. She coughed and there was no syrup or soothing words. There were muffled sounds in the house, but no one came when she called. She dozed to wake and find it was still night and dozed again. In the middle hours of the morning she got up and found there was no chamber-pot under the bed. She sat on the floor and cried at the thought of going to the Double-U in the cold and dark. It was right down by the back fence, "not easy of access," as Meredith said, "but very

28

nice and private." However, on venturing, she discovered that Grandfather was already up. Lamplight glowed through the kitchen window and the hurricane-lamp was alight, hanging on its post by the back steps. She took it and set off, barefooted, in an outgrown flannelette nightie which reached to her knees. There was frost on the planks which formed the path; stars glittered ice-blue through cold blue air. Gaining sanctuary she stood the lantern on the floor and was reasonably comfortable once the seat warmed a little.

She sang "There's a rose that grows in no-man's land," and went on to "A-N-Z-A-C", "Temple Bells", and "Larboard Watch". She knew all the words.

Happy once more, she returned to the house, hung the lantern on its post and went to the kitchen. The fire was blazing in the stove, kettle lids clattered as they lifted and fell, steam rose from the big, black pots. Grandfather sat in the wicker chair by the stove, fully dressed from his cap to his elastic-sided boots. When he saw her he put his fingers to his lips and whispered, "Get right back to bed and stay there."

But in the warmth of the kitchen, the lamplight and firelight winking back from the brass hooks of the dresser and reflected in the dark, polished linoleum, she began to cough and shiver. He lifted her to his knee, tucked her under the fold of his coat, took her feet in his hands and rubbed them before holding them to the blaze of the fire. She felt contentment rising from her feet all through her and began to grow drowsy.

She woke when Grandfather shook her. It was now daylight. The lamp was out, but the fire blazed brighter than ever. Nurse Truelass was at the stove, pouring hot water into jugs.

"Baby's come," she said, her broad, red face creased in a smile, the steam on her glasses making her blink.

"What baby?" asked Tansy.

"Your mother's baby. Now, isn't that a surprise for you?"

"Why did she want a baby?"

"Everyone likes babies."

"Why?"

"Oh, deary me! Because they do."

"Where did it come from?"

"God sent it."

"Didn't he want it?"

"I can't stand here all the morning arguing with you," said Nurse Truelass; "there's more to do than that." And she went out briskly.

"You've bust my good leg through sleeping on it," said Grandfather, putting her off his knee and rubbing his leg to make it fit to stand upon.

Everyone was busy that morning of the baby. Tansy was told she must not go near the baby or Meredith because of the whooping cough. "Run out in the sun and play till Uncle Joe comes," said Aunt Jessie. "And whoop as much as you want to, but don't think I'll come running."

"I can't help whooping, Aunt Jessie."

So she went out into the bright morning sunshine not pleased with life, nor babies, nor mothers in the front bedroom unable to be seen. It was a pretty day, all blue and gold, with little white puffy clouds skimming across the sky, the clover in the paddock pale-green and tender, the smell of damp dark earth pungent and clean after the frost of the night before; but Tansy found no consolation in it.

She could usually entertain herself. Meredith had put planks to make a path to the Double-U to keep their feet dry in wet weather. One of Tansy's games was to hop from one end to the other on these. Grandfather had taught her. One day while sitting on the back steps he had said, "Bet you can't hop to the dunny and back."

"Bet I can!" and off she set. It had taken several days to get it perfect and then she was rewarded with a raspberry drop, warm and sticky from the bag in Grandfather's pocket. After that they had played it often.

But the whooping-cough had made her weak. Today she set off several times, failed, and to mark each failure sat in the clover and cried. She had started the day crying for lack of a chamber-pot. She had cried when Aunt Jessie gave her bread and treacle for breakfast instead of the boiled eggs she wanted. It seemed as if she was going to spend the day that way. She tried riding on the clothes-prop. Then she went to the fowl house.

They used to have twelve white leghorns in full lay, but they had been stolen last show time. The nests were still there and Tansy liked to crawl in and crow and cackle, being a hen and rooster by turns. But today she was so drowned in tears she could neither crow nor cackle.

She now went to the front of the house and climbed on the post of the front gate. She began to sing "When the sands of the desert grow cold". She liked the sound of it. She sang it over and over. Soon she was quite happy.

Some time later she was still on the gatepost singing "The sands of the desert" when Uncle Joe Sprockett drove up in his sulky. He tied the reins round the board of the sulky and jumped down.

Tansy was mostly pleased to see Uncle Joe, who didn't take bringing her up as seriously as Aunt Jessie did. As a good husband he obeyed Aunt Jessie's bidding when told to scold, but he mostly winked so that only Tansy could see, at the same time. But today she eyed him warily and continued singing instead of saying hullo.

"Hear someone's got a little sister," he said.

She didn't interrupt her singing to answer this nonsense.

"What do you think of the baby?"

"You can have it."

"My! My! Someone in a paddy! Don't you want it?"

"No." And she went on singing. She wasn't interested in a baby which could not be seen.

However, Uncle Joe scooped her off the post, tossed her in the air and caught her, Tansy emitting a bark as he did so.

"Have to stop that, where you're going."

This caught Tansy's interest. "Why, where am I going, Uncle Joe?"

"Land's End, that's where you're going."

"Land's End?"

"Said so, didn't I? You'll find before you're many hours older that Joe Sprockett is a man of his word."

"Land's End," murmured Tansy. She knew about Land's End. Meredith had told her. Granny and Grand-dad Trenworth were there. Granny and Grand-dad and the Sawpit Tree!

4 They set out early in the afternoon for Land's End, which was "A long way there and a long way back", according to Uncle Joe.

Tansy did not see Meredith before she left. Of all things she was asleep, though she had often said that sleeping in the day-time was a bad habit. She had often said, also, "What would I do without you?" in regard to Tansy. Very well. She had brought this on herself.

As they were about to start Nurse Truelass came to the door and held up a bundle.

"That's it," said Uncle Joe.

Tansy looked but was not impressed. It hardly seemed the sort of thing which would be of any use to Meredith in her stead.

"Gee-up," said Uncle Joe, and off they went, along the street, round the corner, and up past Hogan's where several Hogan children, including the boy who brought the milk, were playing marbles beside the road. Soon they passed Uncle Joe's and Aunt Jessie's own house.

"No use calling, looks as if they're out," said Uncle Joe, who liked making this sort of remark. "See this road?" He pointed ahead with his whip. "It would take you straight to

Derrick Plains if you was going all the way. As there's not much to see in front for some time, kneel up and look backwards and watch the town roofs out of sight."

Uncle Joe was unaware that Meredith's instructions to Tansy in sulkies was "sit back, keep your legs out straight and hang on". Uncle Joe, all round, had a much more permanent idea of life than Meredith.

When the roofs had disappeared and she was facing the right way again they were in a belt of trees, stringy-bark gums.

"I always know when your grand-dad is coming to town," said Uncle Joe as they went through them, "I see the white hood of the Ford above this belt. I tell Jess and she puts a white sheet on the line to let your mother know the Land's End folks are on the way in."

"Oh," Tansy said. When Granny and Grand-dad were coming Meredith always suddenly had a feeling and popped scones in the oven, with which she surprised them when they arrived. Tansy had been proud of the accuracy of her mother's feelings in this matter and did not care for Uncle Joe's version.

Aunt Jessie often said that her Joe could talk the legs off the kitchen table and having only Tansy for an audience did not stop him. He told the history of each place they passed. That was Ferguson's, that MacDonald's, Quinlan's back behind there. And now they were coming along to the river, the Condamine. No, he didn't think Tansy had seen this part of it before. The Condamine always had water in it just here. Tansy leant over the sulky wheel to look at the water as they rattled over the bridge, expecting to feel Uncle Joe's restraining hand on the back of her dress any minute. But Uncle Joe did no such thing.

"Look along there," said Uncle Joe. "That's the old Cuthbertson place." Tansy looked and saw the small, grey slab house where Cuthie and Pap had lived till recently. It was occupied, smoke rising from the chimney, the garden trim. But there was a new house going up behind it, away from the river.

"Going to leave it to itself, I see," said Uncle Joe. "There'll be only the ghosts of the little fellows. She saw them herself, you know, Mrs Cuthbertson did, sitting side by side on the stool by the fire in their nightshirts, the way they were that night, gold curls in ringlets from their tubbing, cheeks rosy from the fire. Eating bread and milk, their last meal on this mortal earth. I know for I was there.''

''That was the flood,'' said Tansy, who had heard Meredith tell the story of how her two brothers were drowned the year before she herself was born. But Uncle Joe's stories were better than Meredith's.

''The ninety-two flood,'' said Uncle Joe. ''Came up sudden the river that night. We all went up on the barn roof. Made us as comfortable as she could, Mrs Cuthbertson did. But not much use trying. Rain pouring, river rising, wind howling. And what made it more eerie-like was that now and again the moon shone down from a rift in the clouds. Just for a second. Full moon it was. Near Easter. The Easter moon. And it never lit a more desolate scene.'' Tansy felt her throat aching. This was a sad story which always brought tears.

''Everything grey,'' went on Uncle Joe. ''Not even the moon could make it anything else. The rain grey and the river water and the half-drowned willows on the river bank. And the faces of the watchers,'' he said impressively.

''And everything swirling. The rising water, the rain, the willow branches. And hair whipped back from human heads. You only saw it for a second, mind. Then the moon went out and the darkness came down, blacker than ever.''

''The hurricane-lamp had gone out too,'' supplied Tansy.

''Of course it had,'' said Uncle Joe, impatient at the interruption. ''Hurricanes will stand a fair bit, but not that much. The strange thing was that the boys were there that night and not safe at Land's End as they should have been. But a few days previously your Granny had been down on a visit to her mother and father and the little fellows begged to stay with their grandparents, as little fellows do. She went home taking

Maggie and Kate with her, leaving Eddie and Johnnie behind."

Uncle Joe sighed heavily and tugged at his moustache with one hand while the other slackened on the reins. The horse slowed to a walking pace, pausing now and again to nibble at a patch of grass beside the road.

"All through the night Mrs Cuthbertson kept calling, 'Eddie, Johnnie, are you safe?' I fancy I hear her voice still. 'Yes, Cuthie, we're here.' She answered, 'Hang on, boys, hang on; soon it will be morning.' But they must have fallen asleep. She called and there was no answer. In the morning they were gone, their little bones together somewhere, no one knows where."

The banking tears overflowed and chased one another in large drops down Tansy's cheeks.

"Here, what's the sunshower about? Gee-up, Roany." To cheer her up he went on to tell how with this, and another little fellow dying as a baby, Meredith running off with George, and Maggie and Kate marrying and going to live in other districts, Granny and Grand-dad Trenworth had had little use of their children. But Tansy found this sad too, and cried harder, causing Uncle Joe concern. She had never cried so much on one day in all her life.

The road and the river ran side by side now. They followed the road till they came to a signpost, where Uncle Joe stopped. He pointed his whip along the road ahead. "To Derrick Plains," he said. "Ah! You wouldn't know it now. Cut up in small chunks, four, five hundred acres, outsiders on 'em. The Man Himself would turn in his grave if he knew. Know who The Man Himself was?"

Tansy shook her head.

"Jeremy Grant Whittaker," said Uncle Joe impressively.

"Ah," she said reverently. She had heard of Jeremy Grant Whittaker and pictured him as a huge figure, with a long white beard like Grandfather's, and a halo round his head. In

35

Tansy's mind's eye he was forever caught in a moment of time as he stepped out of the hills with his sheep before him.

"He came to be known as The Man Himself because he took up his land and worked it instead of putting a manager on it and living far off just collecting his money," said Uncle Joe.

"But ah" — Uncle Joe sighed as heavily as he had when about to tell of Eddie and Johnnie — "those foolish grand-children of his! Built up something for them and all they got was high notions! Sold the land for money to live in the cities. They've all come low by living high. It's the way of it.

"Two, three months back a young fellow comes up to me. I look at him and I think, I know you, sonny, you're one of them, you've got The Man Himself's mark on you. But differ-ent, oh, different! Sure enough, he calls me Uncle Joe. 'Uncle Joe,' he says, 'lend me a fiver.' Now a five pound note is a lot of money. Me and Jess could live a month or more on that. But I gave it to him. What else could I do, though I'll never set eyes on it again? What would The Man Himself think if I hadn't?"

"He's dead," said Tansy.

Uncle Joe frowned. "Makes no difference. He's turning in his grave on account of them and keeping a weather eye out from up there if I know him."

Uncle Joe pointed his whip first at the ground, then at the heavens. Tansy's eyes followed the whip while she marvelled at the versatility of the dead.

Uncle Joe sighed again and whipped up. "I don't know what will come of the whole bunch of them. The Man Himself so different, so very different."

Tansy sighed too, but only to let Uncle Joe know she was sympathetic. She didn't feel as badly about this as she had about Eddie and Johnnie. She was not feeling much about any-thing. The last lot of tears and the afternoon sunshine had put her into a trance-like state through which Uncle Joe's voice penetrated clearly, but as if he were talking to someone else.

They turned off the road onto a track. Trees appeared. One here, one there, then a group together.

Roany went smartly along the winding track. Clip-clop, went his hooves, clip-clop, and echoes came back from among the trees. His tail swished. Dust rose. The sulky swayed from side to side. Uncle Joe's voice rose above the echoing hoof-beats.

"A bit of real scenery, this road through to Land's End."

"Pretty," murmured Tansy.

Uncle Joe turned and looked at her. "Don't tell me you're going to sleep? Now I'll tell you something. Catherine Trenworth, your granny, is a good woman, but she don't hold with sleeping at the wrong time. The sun is getting down a bit," conceded Uncle Joe, "but it still won't do for you to go to sleep."

"I'm not asleep, Uncle Joe."

"I'd advise you to stop that way. Now, to keep you awake, I'll tell you about The Man Himself and how your Great-grand-dad came to settle here. Fine, steady man he was, old Trenworth, head shepherd on Derrick Plains from the beginning. And there some years when The Man Himself comes to him one day and says, 'You're too good a man to be a shepherd all your life, Billy. With all those childer you'll need something for them. Take up land of your own, man, though sorry I'll be to lose you.'

"Now old Billy was getting seven and sixpence a week and rations, so he says, 'How does a poor man do that, Boss?'

" 'Why, man, I'll stake you,' says The Man Himself, clapping him on the shoulder, 'and good luck to you. I've got a piece in my mind's eye. It abridges here. Your childer and mine will flourish side by side.' Ah, little he knew!

"So Billy goes home to his wife Jenny and gathers the childer about them. He tells how it is. Says he, 'It's bushbread and molasses from now on. If the molasses is done before quarter's end, it's boxthorn berries and pigweed. The last is fare good enough to keep alive on, I hear, but I doubt if you'll like it any. Tighten your belts and start now seeing how little you can get by on. And it's work for every man jack of you as is up to it'

— he pointed along the line to Danny, who was four years old — 'and for the others as they grow to it, from sun-up till dark, for there won't be no fat for the slush-lamp. That will be needed to keep the rust from the saws and sledges.'

"It was The Man Himself told me that story. And he says to me, he says, 'You can see for yourself, Joe, what Billy Trenworth made of it. I never helped a better man'.

"To show what The Man Himself was, this land was going cheap. It had been a grant to a town fellow who came up once and was scared off by the mopokes and dingoes and a few poor, naked, skinny Blacks who held the waterhole by tribal right for their full-moon sheenanikins. To this day the shells of the oysters the Blacks brought are by the waterhole. And that's another story I can tell you of The Man Himself. While everyone was treating the Blacks as Blacks —"

But what it was The Man Himself treated the Blacks as, Tansy never found out. The trees fell away. They were in the clearing before the home paddock.

There by the eastern gate was the tall pine she had heard Meredith speak about. Ahead was a long, low house, the late afternoon sun reflected in its windows. Beside it was a line of orange trees. Yes, she knew. Great-aunt Carrie Trenworth, Grand-dad's sister, had planted the trees before she died. Inside the three-strand fence was the shearers' hut. Down in the corner were the cowbails, two cows standing near swishing their tails. Sunlight fell in golden streaks across the yellow grass of the home paddocks. The dam was a sheet of fire. She saw the windmill and a flock of brightly coloured birds flash up from the trough. Sheep in a nearby paddock turned and wheeled away, raising dust. It was all as Meredith had told her so often. She was wide awake now.

"Where is it, Uncle Joe, where is it?"

"Where's what?"

"The Sawpit Tree."

"That's it, that old box-tree you can see beyond the barn."

The branches of the Sawpit Tree were spread out against the

late afternoon sky. She looked and looked at it. Under the Sawpit Tree Meredith had met George, and here was Tansy — home to Land's End at last.

The sulky stopped. Uncle Joe threw the reins to Tansy, jumped down and opened the gate.

"Gee-up, Roany," he called. Uncle Joe did not get back into the sulky but walked at Roany's head, so it was Tansy who drove herself up to the gate in the white paling fence which surrounded her granny's house.

Granny, who came running down the steps, wiping her hands on her large white apron, saw nothing unusual in the circumstance.

Granny was like Cuthie in appearance, except that where Cuthie's once golden hair was now silver, Granny's was only beginning to fade. Tansy had heard much about her granny's hair, which could be sat upon when she let it down at bedtime to make it into two thick plaits for the night. By day it was in swathes about her head, piled high. She had Cuthie's china blue eyes and white skin. She was tall, like Cuthie, but was stouter in build and had a setness and stillness about her which Cuthie did not.

Though Cuthie's daughter and eighteen years younger, habits of mind made her appear older than Cuthie. Catherine Trenworth had been born grown-up, Tansy had heard Cuthie say. She had married young and when still a girl had become mistress of Land's End, taking on also the responsibility of Grand-dad's old and ailing parents, and having in quick succession the children who had been so little use to her in later life.

All this Tansy had heard in some form or other, but it had had no reality for her until now. Granny, on infrequent visits to town, had been kind to her in a brisk, stand-offish way. It had hardly felt to Tansy that Granny had anything to do with her.

It was only now that both Cuthie and Granny came into real

focus in her mind, their relation to one another, to Meredith and herself. Cuthie, Granny, Meredith, Tansy. It surprised her. Though she had known in a way, though Meredith had spoken of them often, Grandfather's more hearty stories of the Strathallans had overshadowed her mother's people. Anne-Margaret beyond the stars had been more real than Cuthie or Granny. But in the last few weeks Cuthie had made her presence felt and now here was Granny, large as life. Tansy was unsure whether the relationship was going to be to her liking or not. She smiled at Granny, said "Hullo," but without success.

"What is it, Joe? What is it?" asked Granny.

"Don't fret, Catherine. All's well. The baby's there and both doing nicely. But someone had the whoops and Jess and me and Mrs Cuthbertson thought this the best place to bring her."

"You acted right, Joe. If I'd known, she'd have been here before, despite Meredith's touchiness about her. Nothing like this air for whoops or complaints of the chest."

"How she got the whoops," said Uncle Joe, "is a long story which can be told another time."

"Oh, I see," said Granny, "up to something again! I may be wrong, Joe, but I fancy I can cure that, too."

"I think you can indeed, Catherine," said Uncle Joe gravely. "None better in my opinion. Now you'll want to hear news of Mr Cuthbertson. And I'm sorry to say there's nothing I can tell you that would be a comfort."

"Is he suffering?"

Uncle Joe looked at her sadly.

"That's the hard part, Joe," said Granny. "To the other I'm resigned by now. It comes to us all in the end. You'll stay the night?"

"No, I'll get along after the meal. Jess is timid-like in the house at night."

Uncle Joe lifted Tansy from the sulky and set her on the ground. Her legs were stiff and she fell over.

Granny regarded her. "Best get up," she said at last; "not much use your stopping there."

Uncle Joe had Tansy's carry-all. She expected Granny to take her hand, but she didn't. They went through the gate and along a brick path to the front steps, then along the verandah and crossed a landing which led to the kitchen.

The kitchen was nearly as big as Tansy's whole house at home. There was a deeply recessed fireplace with a large stove. A long table stood in the middle of the room with forms either side and a chair each end. A large dresser took up one wall. There was a bunk under a wooden window. Tansy immediately climbed upon it. She opened the window. Ah yes! There were the grapevines under which Meredith had played as a little girl.

"Close that and stop meddling," said Granny.

"The gravevines," she said.

"So?"

"They're still there."

"Of course. Where else would they be?"

Granny set the cloth on the long table. It was white, stiffly starched, covered from end to end with red drawn-thread. "We'll make tea an hour on, Joe, for you to get back," she said. Tansy was to find that only occurrences of unusual nature put anything forwards or backwards at Land's End.

Uncle Joe stood in the doorway, drooped a little, his head being higher than the door-ledge. "I take that kindly, Catherine." A pleased smile hovered under his moustache as he watched the food going on the table.

Tansy watched too. There were hot things under covers, spiced steak, liver, pork sausages out of tins, eggs and bacon, gravies, bubble-and-squeak. Then there were cold meats, bread and buns, sauces and pickles and jams.

"You don't have boxthorn berries and pigweed here any more, Granny," she said conversationally.

"I should think not," said Granny; "never did have to my knowledge. Ring the cowbell for your grand-dad, child." She reached to the ledge above Uncle Joe's head and handed down the bell. Tansy went to the verandah. The bell made only a tinkling sound but it echoed loud and clear out over the silent, darkening paddocks.

"Now get a chair and put the bell back where it came from."

There was a chair by the door and Tansy pushed it over and climbed up. She got down and was careful to put the chair back, looking through her eyelashes at Granny to see if she noticed her goodness. She didn't.

Grand-dad came quickly. They heard him out by the tank washing his face and hands. Then he came in, looking from one to the other of the three of them. "Not Pap. Baby come," he said.

Grand-dad was tall and thin with smooth brown skin and deep blue eyes. He had bushy black eyebrows, a long black moustache and was bald, apart from a strip of black hair which ran down the back of his head from ear to ear.

"Sit you down, Joe," said Granny.

They all sat, then everyone bowed their heads so Tansy bowed hers and Granny, in tones like those of the Rector when he had christened Tansy, said:

> "Be present at our table, Lord;
> Thou art here and everywhere adored;
> These victuals bless and grant that we
> May come to feast in Paradise with Thee."

She raised her head and said in her ordinary voice, "Fall to, Joe."

Uncle Joe did, Granny and Grand-dad with him. Tansy was hungry and thought she did nicely, but Granny wasn't satisfied. "She's a picker. We'll soon settle that."

As soon as the meal was finished Uncle Joe prepared to depart. They stood on the verandah and watched till the hurricane-lamp at the back of the sulky disappeared amongst the trees. The night was dark and silent, crispy, frosty crackle in the air, the white stars winking. It seemed to Tansy a long time since she had sat crying on the floor of the little back room that morning.

"I won't be coming inside tonight," Granny said to Grand-dad. He went into one of the sitting-rooms and, before he closed the door after him, Tansy caught a glimpse of shining furniture and a fire burning in a small black stove. The swinging lamp had been burning low; he turned it up and yellow light flooded the windows, showing the pattern of the lace curtains. Tansy and Granny returned to the kitchen and soon the strains of a concertina came to them.

She was tired. "I think I'll go to bed now, Granny."

"What about the washing-up?" demanded Granny. She handed her a tea-towel. "What! Not wiped up before? Thought not. Time you learnt. The best time for learning anything is now."

So her granny washed up and she wiped and when Granny had finished her part, Tansy still had a long way to go. "No good looking at me," said Granny. "I've plenty to occupy me in the meantime." She went off leaving Tansy there. She went round the verandah with stone bottles filled with hot water. She trimmed the wick of a lamp, filled it with kerosene and went off with that, too. She took the big dish from the fire-place, removed the cloth covering it, turned the dough out on the table, punched it hard then put it back in the dish which she reset in the fireplace.

She went outside and came back with a large iron tub which she put in front of the stove.

"Finished? About time too. You'll have to learn to get a bustle on." She tipped the water from the draining tray into the washing-up dish, went outside and threw the water on the geraniums. The *plop* went echoing into the night. Back inside, she took clean water and sandsoap and scrubbed the top of the pot cupboard and the big table. She looked at the gleaming kitchen floor critically. "Mop over have to do it for now," she said. I don't always let things go like this, but there are times when one pair of hands aren't enough.

"Now," said Granny and took up Tansy's carry-all. She began taking out garments, holding them up one by one. "Hmmm," she said again. Bottom-length skirts for little girls were then fashionable. Meredith, however poor, was always fashionable. She found the shrunken flanelette nightie and held it against Tansy. "Won't do," Granny said and put it in the bag where she put things which were to be washed for dusters. "Believe I still have one of your mother's." Away she went to return with a flannel nightgown, long-sleeved, high-collared, heavily embroidered with red feather-stitch.

There was a little tank attached to the side of the stove and she emptied the hot water from this into the tub, took off Tansy's guernsey and print frock, which left her in cotton singlet and Vees. She turned her round and pinched each side of her bottom protruding from the Vees. "Cold as doom," she said.

She put her hand up into Tansy's hair holding it up from her neck. Tansy had curly hair uncut from babyhood. Granny stared at it thoughtfully for a while, reached down scissors from the mantelpiece and snipped it off close to her head. Then into the tub Tansy went and was scrubbed from head to toe. When she was out of the bath and Granny was rubbing at her with a hard towel, she said, "What is it? Girl or boy?"

Tansy had forgotten the baby. It took her a while to think. Uncle Joe's words came back. "It's a sister."

"As well," said Granny. "A boy might have taken after Someone Else. Speaking for myself I hope there is going to be no more nonsense."

Tansy nodded wisely.

"I believe you're nearly asleep. As a rule we don't go to bed here till eight, but tonight Grand-dad and I will excuse you."

It was as well. It seemed as if that soft feather bed, with its flannelette sheets warm from the hot bottles, reached up and drew Tansy down and wrapped its arms about her.

Granny blew out the lamp. "Don't cough. Don't call out in the night. Don't wet the bed," she said.

44

Far away the concertina played.

Tansy woke to the full glory of the sawpit tree. It was framed in her doorway, the sunlight shining on its leaves, blue sky showing as its branches stirred in the morning breeze. Magpies carolled.

Her little room had the bed, a wardrobe, chest-of-drawers and a washstand. There was bright pink linoleum on the floor, a crocheted woollen rug beside the bed. The walls and roof were of cypress pine which had gone a sheeny, honey colour with the years. Dark notches made eyes and interesting whorls upon it. In time she was to dig some of them out and receive due punishment.

There were pictures on the walls, photographs of family groups, framed prints given free with Christmas issues of the *Sydney Mail*, and a painting. Lying in her bed, sunlight falling on the painting, she was able to give it her full attention. It was of a farm, a low stone house, stone out-buildings, small paddocks fenced with stones. The stones were grey, the crops green, the soil purple. There were cows in a lane, a horse, fowls and geese. On one side were red cliffs, white gulls upon them, and a bright blue sea cut off in the middle of a wave.

Granny came bustling in looking neat and well washed, her hair up at this early hour of the day, a time when Meredith wore her kimono and slippers and her hair in plaits.

"What, still abed! Grand-dad's up with the milk this long time. At your age I'd have been to the four-mile fence and back by now."

Tansy pointed at the picture. "It's pretty."

"It's pretty and it's true," said Granny. "It was made by your great-grand-aunt Polly as a parting gift to your great-grand-dad and is of the farm outside St Just-in-Penwith in Cornwall, where he was born. It's painted on tin to make it wear, and wear it has, as you can see, only three dints to show its long trip by the Cape."

Tansy knew a cape as a loose coat without sleeves and fancied for a long time that Great-grand-dad had arrived in Australia in such a garment, the painting under his arm.

"The pity of it was," went on Granny, "that it was early spring when it was painted." She pointed out a few pale blossoms in the garden and lane. "Only snowdrops and the first primroses blooming. Later, in high summer, there would have been hydrangeas making a glorious mass of colour along here. Now, out of that bed. A bed is for night, not daytime."

She poured water from the jug into the basin and put out a black-and-white checked print dress. The hem had been let down and a band of black stitched round the bottom. After she left, Tansy put on her clothes and daddled her fingers in the ice-cold water. Then Granny came back with the slop bucket. She inspected both the chambers sitting side by side on the ledge of the washstand.

"Didn't pass anything during the night, I see."

"No, Granny. I didn't feel like it."

"Hardly a reason. I hope there's nothing amiss. Did you say you had washed?" She gave the water in the dish close scrutiny.

"Yes."

"Hmmm." Granny took the flannel, soaped it well and subjected Tansy's face, neck, ears and hands to a good rubbing. After that Tansy always took the precaution of soaping the water and wetting the flannel.

Tansy could hardly wait for breakfast to finish so that she could run off and see for herself those things of which she'd heard tell. But after breakfast was the washing-up, and by the time she'd finished her part of it Granny was already preparing tea for morning smoko, which resulted in wiping-up again. Then Granny said she must sit to the table with her and do twice-times and her letters. She couldn't follow twice-times at all, and after she had made a line of very shaky A's Granny said it was as she'd feared; they must start at the beginning with pothooks. These were rather better, though Tansy found it hard not to add more interesting decoration of her own. While

Granny watched her pothooks she was preparing dinner, which they had at twelve. More washing-up. Then they all had to lie on their beds for an hour.

This first afternoon when Granny rose from her nap she said, "In future at this time we will do a little plain sewing. But now I have to write off to T.C. Beirne's." So Tansy sat beside her while she did this. She heard so much of T.C. Beirne's during her stay at Land's End that she thought they were part of the family. As it happened, T.C. Beirne's was a large store in Brisbane. Much larger than Mr Chaseling's in Goombudgerie, Granny said.

Granny wrote off for: "A bolt of holland; a bolt of navy galatea; a bolt of medium calico; a bolt of warm red flannel; a dozen cotton forty; a dozen red ingrain; one pound of red wool; one pound of white wool, four-ply; six dozen pearl buttons the size of a shilling; six dozen yards red rick-rack braid; two dozen yards two-inch embroidery; one pair brown buttoned boots; one pair black buttoned boots, size eleven; one natural straw hat; one navy straw hat, mushroom shape, twenty-one inches."

"When that comes," said Granny, "you'll look like a real girl."

They were now up to afternoon smoko. Tansy felt sure that when it was over she could go and see the sawpit tree at close quarters for herself.

But after smoko she was sent for the cows. The cows spent the day at the top of the horse paddock under the shade of a quinine tree and she thought the journey should prove interesting. However, as she was about to set off, with Granny's straw hat upon her head and a long-handled whip held importantly in one hand, Granny said, "Keep your distance from the cows. Even the quietest cow will turn. Your Great-uncle Danny bore to the grave the scar he got as a boy when a Jersey ripped his cheek. And she was the quietest cow you ever did see!" So on her trip for the cows Tansy was more involved with personal safety than the scenery.

The cows knew more about being fetched than she did. When she was halfway up the horse-paddock they came amiably towards her, regarded her with interest and trotted past. She turned and followed well to the rear.

Now the shadows were lengthening and the evening star winked through the branches of the sawpit tree. She had never known such a short day. She would have to learn to get a bustle on.

5 Tansy's first day at Land's End was an off-day: that is there was nothing of special moment. Most days brought their own duties. On Monday, washing day, Tansy cut up soap and minded the copper. She had to see that the fire didn't jump out and get away and when the water bubbled call Granny before it boiled over. On Mondays all the mats came off the big dresser and from sundry other places. There were four clothes lines which made a big square, but without the quick drying in this part of the world her granny would never have been able to get all her things hung out.

Tuesday was ironing day, when it was Tansy's duty to iron the mats from the dresser. Granny put them back as they came from Tansy's hands and it took some time for the day to come when she could be proud of them again.

On baking day Tansy greased the tins. And every week there was a particularly dreadful day when all the china was taken down from the big dresser and from the shelves beside the fireplace to be washed, wiped and restacked again.

But Granny liked this day. On the ledge of the dresser, surrounding the silver cruet, were little jugs and jars and sugar basins, each standing on its own mat. One and all were mementos to Granny of someone who had passed away. As they washed and wiped she told Tansy the history of each one in turn.

"You see this," said Granny, "it was Anne-Margaret's own sugar bowl, and though I never set eyes on her I'm pleased to

48

have it. Your mother brought it to me from Strathlea when she returned home here after Anne-Margaret died and Strathlea, through your grandfather's improvidence, was broken up. Fancy a grown man letting a good property slip through his fingers! As to Meredith, it was time she came home, and she knew it. But she wouldn't stay: she would go to Goombudgerie and set up for herself. If she'd stayed here there wouldn't have been the nonsense which has led up to what it has now. I'd have seen to that.''

"But wasn't there nonsense before, Granny?"

"What do you mean?"

"When Mother was here as a girl and met George under the sawpit tree."

"Indeed! The ideas you have in your head! I'd like to know where you hear them all. Your mother met Somebody better-not-mentioned at the Picnic Races at Derrick Plains, where she shouldn't have been at all, Picnic Races not being the kind of amusement your grand-dad or myself care about. In fact we do not care for amusement at all, never having felt the need for it.''

Granny, with Anne-Margaret's sugar bowl in her hands, went to the kitchen doorway and looked down thoughtfully at the sawpit tree. Beyond the old tree, where the earth was still hollow from the hooves of the horses going round and round, drawing the saw which cut the timber when the house was being built, lay the two dams with the windmill beside them. The water in the dams reflected the pale blue winter sky and the windmill turned slowly in the morning breze. On all sides the paddocks stretched away, the yellow grass cropped close by the heavily-wooled sheep, neat grey fences marching into the distance. Peace lay over the land and on the house itself. Stillness and quiet. Now and again the long drawn out *ba-a-a* of a sheep, a bird's call, the click of the windmill as it turned. It was hard to believe that anything untoward had ever happened at Land's End.

"Your mother was fond of sewing, even as a girl," went on

Granny, "and clever at it. This day she wanted cotton and would take her horse and go to the store at Derrick Plains to get it. She set out in the morning and didn't return till nightfall, saying she'd had to wait for it till the mail came in. But there were these races that day and that was that. I am not one to sit in judgement, but I tell the plain unvarnished truth. Her behaviour that day did not do her credit."

There were grim lines round Granny's mouth as she struggled against indignation. It was still one of the most shameful parts of the whole episode to her that her own daughter had told her lies and that she had accepted the lies. She, who prided herself on seeing and knowing everything!

"But the sawpit tree, Granny?"

"The consequence of the other. Very wicked it was. The next thing she was gone. It's over and done now. *And forgotten*. But it won't happen again in my lifetime. I've kept my eyes well skinned ever since."

"But why, Granny?" asked Tansy, who, knowing Meredith had been the youngest daughter, couldn't see the use of Granny keeping her eyes skinned now.

"Because years roll on quickly and history repeats itself. But I'm ready. Make no mistake about that!" She turned and went back into the kitchen. Tansy followed, a most unaccountable prickly sensation running up and down her spine.

Granny put Anne-Margaret's sugar basin, blue glass with a fluted lid, back on its own red-and-white mat on the dresser. "How Anne-Margaret came by that bowl," she went on briskly, "has to do with the days before Federation, when there was customs duty between the states. There was only the bridge across the MacIntyre separating her from New South Wales, so she used to take the baby across in the go-cart, buy something and bring it back under the baby's covers. Why your mother brought that particular bowl was because of who the baby was when Anne-Margaret got it, which circumstance does not interest me. It has pride of place in memory of Anne-

Margaret herself who appears to have been a good woman, much put upon."

After that Tansy handled Anne-Margaret's bowl with care. It was slippery so she took to interceding with Anne-Margaret in her heavenly abode, to see that nothing happened to it. She had already brought Hetty Cooper's gravy-boat and Aunt Bessie's jam-jar to an untimely end.

Once a week the silver was cleaned, other days only rubbed-up, which Granny regretted, but said, "There is too much round here for mortal hands to do; some things must go."

When Tansy had any spare time she was allowed to wander as she pleased if she did not go near the dams, the waterhole, the dip or the trough, and kept within the area of the home paddock, the horse paddock, the fowl yard, the sheep yard, the graveyard and the ridge. At first she was not adventuresome. As well as skinned eyes, Granny admitted to an invisible pair in the back of her head. Also there was her instinct. She thought of things Tansy might do before Tansy thought of them herself.

According to Granny all illness was something in the system and needed to be worked through. So for the whooping cough Tansy was treated to castor oil, which was called blue-bottle, owing to its coming out of a large blue bottle which stood square and resolute on the mantelpiece above the fireplace. Tansy had blue-bottle for several days in a row, weekdays at that. This did not excuse her from the usual Saturday morning routine. Saturday was blue-bottle day for everyone.

At Land's End there were three Double U's, a Ladies', a Gentlemen's and a Shearers'. The Ladies' and Gentlemen's were at the end of the horse paddock, half a mile away, Gentlemen's facing west, Ladies' east, the width of the paddock between them. Unfortunately the Ladies' had grown public with the march of progress. On the next property the people had built on the south boundary. A bare five miles separated the two houses and a track ran along the reserve fence to it.

This lack of privacy, the knowledge that a sulky or horseman might appear on the track, didn't stop Tansy from leaving the door wide open. She had to. There was a white scrubbed seat with a hole far too large for her and, underneath, her idea of the bottomless pit. Besides, there was a family of frogs which pulsated and stared unblinkingly at her. Also a Double U was a place where snakes allegedly foregathered.

One day last summer the Rector had called and Granny and Grand-dad, as was usual with them on such occasion, dropped what they were doing and sat in their armchairs in the sitting-room to entertain him. But the Rector disappeared. They sat there in silence for some time until even Grand-dad was forced to speak.

"Tarnation take it! Where's durned Rector?"

Granny said she thought he had gone thither. Grand-dad went thither also. What he saw was a closed door and a black-, red-bellied snake coiled on the step with its head bolt upright. He went for his gun, returned, and shot it, then went back to the house and resumed his place in the armchair.

At last the Rector reappeared. "Grass-seed's bad on the ridge, Mrs Trenworth," he said.

Having heard this story Tansy watched the step of the Ladies' carefully.

The Shearers' was close to the shearing shed, because in olden days shearers were wicked men who thought nothing of going there to indulge in the weed. From the top stand which Great-grand-dad, and now Grand-dad took, telltale smoke through the cracks of the door could be seen.

With a Ladies', a Gentlemen's and a Shearers', and the now small population of Land's End, no one had to worry on Saturday that they were keeping anyone else out. The only thing which necessitated getting a bustle on was that it was the day the verandahs were scrubbed — and there were a number of verandahs.

Tansy's whooping cough disappeared. Granny couldn't understand why Meredith had let it hang on so long.

All the days of Grand-dad's life had been filled with working. He was the eldest of the thirteen children of Billy and Jenny Trenworth and had come over the line of hills to the east as a baby in his mother's arms. His childhood had been spent on Derrick Plains. As a growing boy he had come with his family to Land's End, and since then had not spent more than a night away from the place and that rarely. Land's End was his world. He was proud of the house he had helped to build, proud of his neat paddocks and clean flocks. His life was devoted to them.

All day long he was out and about, following the fences, counting the sheep, inspecting the windmills. Sometimes a far puff of smoke showed he had gathered burrs blown in from somewhere else and was burning them to prevent their sticking to the sheeps' backs: sometimes the only indication of his whereabouts was his whistle coming to them on the breeze. Granny would cock her ear and smile when she heard it. While he spoke seldom, he whistled often. His whistle was so clear and sweet it could have been mistaken for a bird's, Granny often said — only the birds here did not whistle in that way. They called and chattered rather than whistled.

When the day was over, the shadows stealing across the paddocks, Grand-dad returned to the house, washed, changed his clothes and had his evening meal. Then he went to the sitting-room where he kept his concertina and his phonograph.

Tansy soon learned to get a bustle on with the evening wiping-up. She was as eager as Granny to be in the sitting-room in time for the opening strains of the concertina, or to hear the voice coming so strangely through the horn of the phonograph. An announcement like " 'In the Gloaming' sung by Will Oakland — Edison-Bell Record", sent a shiver of delight through her.

The sitting-room was small and square, furnished with tables, sofas and straight-backed armchairs. On either side of the fireplace, Granny and Grand-dad sat in their accustomed places. Beside Grand-dad was a small table, on which stood the phonograph. Against the wall opposite was the horsehair sofa on which Tansy sat, Granny considering the heat from fires unhealthful for children. The walls had photographs of relations in orderly rows, those who were living framed in brown, those who had departed framed in black.

If Grand-dad played the concertina he sat in his chair, the concertina against his chest, his chin resting on it, his blue eyes smiling behind his glinting glasses. His feet tapped in rhythm. If he played the phonograph, he stood beside it, his glasses in his hand, looking from one to the other of the photographs on the wall when he wasn't giving the machine the care it seemed to need.

Granny sat with her hands folded in her lap and listened. She always gave her full attention to whatever she was doing. When she listened she listened.

Tansy also listened. While Granny and Grand-dad liked the concertina best, she preferred the phonograph. She picked up the words quickly, which Granny thought strange as Tansy had no memory for twice-times or her letters.

Soon the hour away from the work-a-day world passed. There was bread to be set, clocks to be wound, doors to be locked, the weather had to be inspected to know its promise for the morrow; they must be in bed and the lights out by eight o'clock. It would never do for a passer-by to see a lamp burning at Land's End after that hour. All the days of Grand-dad's life had been filled with working, his nights with sleeping. Which was as it should be, Granny said.

Thanks to Grand-dad's phonograph Tansy now knew all the words of "Love's Old Sweet Song", "Carry Me Back to Old Virginny", and "The Longest Way Round Is the Sweetest Way Home". However, you had to be careful when one sang at Land's End. There was a time and place in Granny's life for singing; a wasted breath could slow up household tasks.

So Tansy sang her songs up in the graveyard, a fenced off portion on the ridge behind the house. She sat in the first fork of the mulberry tree which shaded her Great-grand-dad Trenworth, "William, devoted son, father, husband and friend"; "Jenny, relict of William by two months. In death they are not divided"; "Angelina, daughter of above. 'Suffer the little children to come unto Me, for of such is the Kingdom of Heaven' "; her little Uncle David, who had died naturally as a baby instead of being drowned in a flood as his brothers Johnnie and Eddie were; and her Great-aunt Carrie. Great-aunt Carrie had planted the orange trees to console herself when crossed in love but died as the first blossoms appeared upon them, taking to her grave a shocking scar from the scalding she had received when, at Tansy's age, she had allowed the copper to boil over.

So far, Tansy's only scar was a white curve through cutting her finger to the bone when she was peeling an apple with a buffalo-handled knife. It wasn't anything to blow about, as Granny said.

Tansy sang the songs as she brought in the cows of an afternoon, ever mindful of what happened to Great-uncle Danny. She sang them also sitting on the gatepost waiting for visitors to drive up on second Thursday mornings. Second Thursday was visiting day at Land's End. It had been from the time the place was taken up. Once, on that day, all the countryside had gathered there. But at that time everyone was either on Derrick Plains, or had "come off it" to take up their own places.

Since then many people had died and strangers had replaced them. Like Meredith, Granny did not care for strangers. Visiting day had dwindled to Aunt Cissie and her boys. Sometimes Aunt Cissie's mother came as well, but mostly the old lady sent her excuses. At eighty-odd she was having a little trouble with her legs and reserved her energies for important events like funerals, marriages and Christmas. There were other older people, too, living beyond Derrick Plains, who found it too far to come unless the occasion demanded it. Deaths, not visiting day, saw the largest gatherings at Land's End now.

Tansy enjoyed the sight of Aunt Cissie wrapped in an Assam silk dustcoat, her straw hat tied on by a silk fly-veil knotted under her chin, her two boys on the seat beside her. She gloried in the fit and healthy appearance of Aunt Cissie who had survived the '92 flood. She had fallen out of the tree in which she was sheltering and if someone had not seen her pigtail floating on the water she wouldn't have been here at all.

When she removed her hat Tansy drew as close to her as she could, for the famous pigtail was now wound about her head.

"Good gracious, child! Don't breathe on me."

"I haven't the whoops now, Aunt Cissie."

"I don't like being breathed on, just the same."

Aunt Cissie never knew what it was about her that interested Tansy so much. She brought great bunches to Land's End, the largest sunflowers, the most colourful dahlias, and what Tansy loved best, rosemary, lavender and verbena. She brought also tins of biscuits, fresh beef, home-cured sausages and home-made cheese.

The boys, referred to by Aunt Cissie as her two little men, were eight and nine. They teased Tansy unmercifully, but she followed them everywhere, trotting at their heels in tears. There was the day they went to the forbidden waterhole. They knew Tansy was not allowed, so they dared her to go. Tansy went.

But Granny, her instinct well to the fore, was waiting by the windmill when the three of them came home again.

"Did you go to the waterhole?"

"*She* went," said Aunt Cissie's elder boy, "and we went and brought her home again."

"Yes, we did so," said the younger.

Too taken aback to say anything, Tansy was marched off to bed.

But the following Thursday, miss one, she was back on the gatepost singing "In the Shade of the Old Apple Tree" as a praise offering for Aunt Cissie's aliveness, as she waited for them to appear.

Appear they did, swinging up through the trees, Aunt Cissie Assam-silk-coated, the fly-veil tying on her straw hat, her little men on the seat beside her, her tins and baskets and cloth-wrapped meat with the blood staining through, and flowers at her feet. In the middle of her song Tansy stopped, jumped down and swung wide the gates and they all shouted together as the sulky rattled through. Then Tansy clambered onto the sulky and laughing merrily they drove up to the house.

But five minutes later she would be crying again, and most afternoons found her sent to bed after a virtuously explained crime. It was all very unfair. The unfairness reminded her of her friend Dolores, to whom on no account was she ever to speak again.

She wept for Dolores and for herself and lovely vanished things, to say nothing of the warm gingerbread, hot scones and grape jam being eaten in the kitchen for afternoon smoko.

The parcel from T.C. Beirne took some time to reach them. The river had a habit of rising at times of emergencies or when parcels, important letters, and the Christmas food supply had to be brought over from the other side.

However, it turned up at last and busy days followed while Tansy was refitted. The holland and galatea turned into dresses which reached below her knees and had several tucks to allow for growing. The calico became drawers, stay-bodices and pin-afores, the first two having the embroidery upon them, the third the rick-rack braid. The warm red flannel made petti-coats, the white wool comforters, a prickly garment knitted in garter stitch for wearing against the skin. The red wool became knee-length socks in feather-and-fan pattern.

Thus outfitted she became a quite different little girl. She took on manners and a middle-aged staidness and became a fitting companion for Granny.

She could discuss with her momentous problems such as whether it should be barley or peas in the broth. She could tell her that some people in town bought eggs instead of growing them in their own backyard or having them brought in; as much as a penny was sometimes charged for just one egg. And she could deliver statements such as: "The Knightbridges have a big family. A new baby every six months, I hear."

"I had to wipe my eyes," Granny would tell Grand-dad. "She's so old-fashioned."

As being old-fashioned was what Granny liked best, Tansy gathered that Granny liked her. She was being a success at Land's End. Meredith and that baby in Goombudgerie could do without her as long as they pleased.

At Land's End on Sunday they had a quiet day; six days shalt thou labour, on the seventh rest. After the morning work they put on their best clothes. Grand-dad did not go to the paddocks.

At noon they sat to dinner: fowl and the many things Granny considered necesssary to go with it, and plum pudding. They took their nap, then Grand-dad went to the garage, backed out the Ford and brought it up to the front gate. With Granny and Grand-dad in the front, Tansy behind, they went to the end of the reserve and back.

At afternoon smoko they had cake: rich fruit, plain fruit, sand, madeira, saffron, Dolly Varden, vanity. Afterwards Granny played the organ in the sitting room and they sang hymns. "Shall we Gather at the River", "The Birds Have Their Nests", "Onward, Christian Soldiers", "Rock of Ages", "Nearer My God to Thee", and "Abide with Me" were Tansy's favourites, and she sang them to the cows each Sunday as she brought them in. Also to William and Jenny if darkness didn't fall too soon. "Abide with Me" had been composed in Brixham in Devon. Devon was the next place to Cornwall, so it was Grand-dad's favourite. Granny liked them all and would have been content to play the book through from start to finish.

After tea they had sacred music on the phonograph. "Hallelujah, Hallelujah", "I Know that My Redeemer Liveth", and "The Lord Is My Shepherd".

At eight o'clock Sunday ended. The clocks were wound, the lamps blown out. They were rested, ready to join the hurly-burly of life again on the morrow. And so to bed and the sleep of the just, for Tansy to wake next morning, the sawpit tree framing her doorway, the sun on its branches, the magpies shouting their heads off.

Days flashed by fast at Land's End. They rolled into each other, into weeks, into months. Steadily they bore the inmates of the old homestead on golden wings of sunlight towards that bourne from whence no traveller returns. Granny spoke of it often. With Tansy's natural love of travel she was only too happy to be accompanying Granny and Grand-dad on this journey.

6 There was a spell of bad weather and the river rose. The mail was late. Finally, as the bridge was still under water, it was swum across on horseback.

A black-edged envelope lay on top of the bundle of letters. Granny knew what it was when she saw it. "He has answered the call; his pain is over," she said. Her face crinkled till she looked like an old woman. She turned away from Tansy, standing still for a moment, then turned back, her face composed. "Ring the cowbell for your Grand-dad, dearie," she said as she slit the envelope with steady fingers.

"Is it Pap, Granny?"

"Yes, Tansy, Pap is dead. You have lost a good friend in this world, for all you knew him so little."

Grand-dad came. He and Granny went to change. They came back, Granny in a black dress, heavy jet beads with a silver cross attached, a black scarf tied over her hair, Grand-dad in his dark suit and best hat, which now had a thick band around it.

Pap's photograph was taken from its place on the wall on the left-hand side of the fireplace. (Cuthie's photograph was on the right-hand side.) It was changed into a black frame and placed on the table, a vase of flowers, white geraniums, daisies and maidenhair beside it. The photograph had been taken as a young man, when he had a soft brown beard, smooth cheekbones, laughing eyes, and a high forehead under dark wavy hair.

Granny tied a black ribbon about Tansy's arm. "Go to the gate and open it for Aunt Cissie's and the Brackenridges' traps. There'll be others too. Shut the gate between each one."

Tansy went to the gate and sat on the post, red legs in feather-and-fan dangling. "Pap is dead," she said. She didn't sing. She was bursting with a holy, solemn feeling, there in the sunshine under the blue sky, clean and fresh after the days of rain. She looked up into the sky from where, no doubt, a Pap whose eyes laughed again now he was out of pain, looked down. He could see her and she couldn't see him. Like Granny's instinct, it scared her a little. She tried to remember about Pap, but all that kept popping into her head was Meredith saying he was a dreadful tease.

Then there was the rhyme she often said which Pap had taught her when she was a little girl: "Apple pie without cheese is like a kiss without a squeeze." Hardly suitable to chant at this moment.

Aunt Cissie's sulky came in sight. Uncle Bob was driving, Aunt Cissie on the outside and the two boys squeezed between them. There were tins and baskets and bundles and so many flowers not an inch of space was left. There was no glad shouts today as they rattled through.

Tansy shut the gate but was hardly back on the post when

60

she had to jump down again. This was Mrs Brackenridge, Aunt Cissie's mother. With her in the sulky was her son Tom, his wife and two small children. Two older children rode behind on ponies.

So it went on. By noon all those caught by the river, unable to follow Pap to the grave, who had known him in the olden days, were gathered. There were "strangers", too, neighbours from the little properties along the river. Unlike Meredith and Granny, Pap and Cuthie had never been averse to "strangers". The sulkies rested on their shafts in the shade of the sawpit tree and the horses were loose in the paddock. Harness and halters hung on pegs on the outside of the barn.

The long table in the kitchen was crowded for the midday meal. It was eaten gravely, almost in silence. Then everyone went to the sitting-room. The burial service was read, hymns were sung, then stories about Pap were told.

Pap had been second shepherd on Derrick Plains when Great-grand-dad Trenworth was head shepherd. In time Pap went to the River to his own place, a small property, enough to feed them and get by on, Pap having had enough of damned hard work, having been at it since early boyhood.

Unlike Grand-dad and Granny, Pap and Cuthie found pleasure in other things beside work. Pap was not a landsman; only circumstances had turned him into a shepherd. He came from Lancashire, a cotton man — one of his uncles had invented the Spinning Jenny. The cotton famine had displaced him. "I didn't leave old England; I was booted out by my belly," he always said; a phrase Tansy liked but didn't understand to mean that he had known hunger and privation and had come to Australia to avoid these things.

The stories of Pap weren't of rising in the world and prosperity, but of how he had helped people, the funny way he said things, and his teasing, of which Cuthie was the chief victim. He and Cuthie had come from different spheres of life and didn't see eye to eye about anything. Cuthie, born on the Isle of Wight, had come to London as a child with her family. Her father was a successful architect so "her belly had never stuck to her backbone" and, according to Pap, it was only after such a state of affairs that anyone could see straight.

Cuthie's England and Pap's were two different places. What they had their arguments about were England, the Royal Family, calling England "home", which Cuthie did and Pap did not ("This is home here and I couldn't wish for a better one"), the merits of cooking in the south and north of England, Pap emphatic that the north won — "though I haven't much to go on, God help me" — religion, the existence or otherwise of heaven and hell; the rearing of children; the furnishing of houses; the planting of the garden. By the time all this was thrashed out the day was done.

So, starting with prayers and hymns and ending with gentle laughter, Pap was laid to rest in the hearts of his friends.

They rode away in the late afternoon. Land's End was lonely that evening. The loneliness blew in from the plain. It glimmered down from the stars. It was in the bulk of the sawpit tree, dark against the sky. It echoed from the sacred music Grand-dad played on the phonograph.

Then Granny shook herself. "Best to bed. Tomorrow is another day."

Tomorrow they went forward without Pap. Dear ones came and dear ones went, Land's End and life went on.

A few weeks later there was another letter from town. Though in a black-edged envelope it was of a different nature. It was from Meredith; Granny read it and looked pleased.

"Your mother has returned to her own opinions," she said. "Reading between the lines, I don't think we're going to hear much of Someone-better-not-mentioned in future. She's coming out with the Rector the first Sunday in September. They're bringing the baby to be christened here where it should be christened. Cuthie will be with her and is to be a godparent, myself another, Grand-dad another. I wonder why Cuthie?

She can't last till the baby's grown to do her duty by her. Aunt Cissie would have been more suitable."

"Aunt Cissie is of another persuasion," Tansy said.

"That's right. I forgot. Aunt Cissie and I rarely speak of religion." She referred to the letter again. "The baby is to be called Mary Caroline, after Cuthie, I see. Your mother and Cuthie must have grown thick as thieves since Pap went. It wasn't my opinion previously that Meredith and Cuthie got on. Cuthie is downright and untroubled by other people's susceptibilities, unlike Meredith. I have some myself," admitted Granny.

"What's a susceptibility, Granny?" asked Tansy.

"It's having corns that can be trodden upon," replied Granny. "Cuthie maintains that I spoilt Meredith. I have never spoiled anyone. But as things turned out the way they did it was possible to take that view. Cuthie took it. I have forgiven her, of course, years ago.

"Another thing I have forgiven was her allowing the children to call her 'Cuthie'. She would not be called anything sensible like Granny. She did not like being a granny at all, a most unnatural view. I was liable, as a young woman, to become worked up by Cuthie, even though she was my own mother. I'm not saying she wasn't a good mother. She was the best, but she was apt to vaunt unsuitable ideas. It came of being brought up in England when a new era was dawning. It's my opinion that women have a place and should stay there."

Tansy was enjoying this conversation. "Cuthie thinks I'm ugly," she said to keep it going.

"Not ugly, just plain, which is best for a girl," said Granny absently, referring to the letter again. "Your Grandfather Strathallan calls the baby 'Marny' and this name has stuck. I must say your mother hardly knows her own mind when she's naming children."

"Does Grandfather like the baby?" Tansy asked.

"She doesn't say, but I daresay he does. No one can resist a baby."

"I bet it can't hop to the dunny and back."

"Did I hear you aright? What did you say?"

"Can it walk?" Tansy murmured.

"I am willing to let some things go, considering circumstances and the strides you have made of late. No; of course it can't walk. It's only two months old. Now we must get a bustle on to have the place looking its best by the first Sunday in September."

When Grand-dad came in to dinner Granny told him what was in Meredith's letter. Surprisingly he said something: "Wonder what she's like, t'little lass?"

"I have a feeling she's a very nice baby," said Granny.

Tansy looked at her hoping she was going to say "as Someone-else was"; but all she added was, "Those who want praise to their face don't get it."

The days wheeled away. Not much time to sing to Jenny and William, or sit on the gatepost. Twice her letters and plain sewing were forgotten altogether. The roofs and walls were scrubbed, floors polished, curtains and bedspreads starched and ironed. The silver was done every day, not just rubbed-up.

"There are times when a body needs more than one pair of hands," said Granny.

The peach trees broke into blossom, the fat mauve stocks in the garden bloomed, the leaves of the sawpit tree shone in the sunshine, little white lambs dotted the paddocks, the breeze blew pleasantly over all the land.

They came to the baking days, and as Granny mixed and Tansy greased tins, or picked the stalks from currants, or stood by with another egg ready to break in, they hoped and hoped to each other that the river would stay down.

"Even snow on those mountains down south does it," said Granny.

"Is it real snow like the London snow that used to fall on Cuthie's tippet?" asked Tansy.

"S'pect so. Never seen any of it myself; nor do I wish to.

Bad in Lancashire, you know, the snow. The women wear shawls over their heads to keep it off. So far north.''

"Isn't north hot?''

"Not in England. We're bottom to endways of England.''

The morning came when Tansy, as stiffly starched as the curtains and bedspreads, sat on the gatepost singing "There is a Green Hill Far Away'', because it was Sunday. It was a day of unusual occurence at Land's End; dinner was an hour back as the Rector couldn't leave town till after matins.

Shortly after midday the Rector drove up in his Chevrolet. Beside him in front was his schoolboy son, Hubert, and in the back Meredith and Cuthie and the baby.

Tansy had hardly realised how fond she was of Meredith till she saw that dear, familiar black-and-white checked costume again. They waved as they went through the gates and after she closed the gates she went running, knowing Meredith would watch to catch her in her arms as soon as possible.

But mothers are surprising people. There she had been without Tansy for several months and she didn't even let the baby go to catch her, but bent to kiss her with it in her arms. "Steady, Tansy, don't hurt Marny.'' She straightened up and laughed. "You look as if you had stepped out of a photograph. What do you think of her, Cuthie?''

"You can't beat Catherine,'' said Cuthie; "she does not move with the times.''

Marny was held out for Tansy's inspection. She was swathed in shawls and her bonnet was over one eye, the strings in her mouth with her fist. One bursting pink cheek and one very blue eye showed. "You may hold her later,'' said Meredith.

"No, thank you. I might drop it. I dropped Aunt Bessie and Hetty Cooper.''

"Good heavens! Did you? And you're alive to tell the tale. Things have changed since my day.''

Meredith was different somehow. Brisker. She looked younger, and her face, which Tansy used to think looked sad, was no longer so. She was quite cheerful. With the spotted veil of her sailor hat thrown back, the tendrils of hair escaping on her forehead gave her a rakish air. From the lobes of her neat little ears hung tiny jewelled earrings.

While Meredith bent her green inquiring look on Tansy, Tansy looked just as inquiringly at the earrings. Previously the only jewellery Meredith had worn was her plain gold wedding ring. George's presents had lain unheeded in the sandalwood box on the dressing table. Now she laughed gaily and put her hand up to her ear. The earring tinkled.

At that moment Granny came hurrying down the steps wiping her hands on her apron. "Welcome all," she said. "Your Reverence and Boy." She shook hands with the Rector and Hubert, kissed Cuthie and Meredith, took Marny from Meredith's arms. "This is a day I'm happy to see, Meredith."

"I would have had it otherwise. But what is, is."

"That's right, my girl. I'm glad you see it that way at last. We'll make the best of things in our own fashion."

In Granny's bedroom Marny was placed on the bed, unswathed from her shawls and admitted to be a beautiful baby. Grand-dad bent over her a long time, raised himself and said, "She's fine, t'little lass," and went out.

Attention was removed from the baby by Cuthie's taking off her black satin hat. Granny clasped her hands in front of her. "Mother!" she exclaimed.

"I had it bobbed," said Cuthie, fluffing up the soft, silver remains of the hair before the dressing-table mirror.

"But what would Pap have said? It was your crowning glory!"

"Crowning glory or not," said Cuthie, "it made a fine mess on the barber's floor. As to that foolish old man of mine, he was the last to want a woman to carry round a cartload of hair all her days."

"I wouldn't sacrifice mine," said Granny.

"You seem to have sacrificed Someone-else's."

"That was different; it needed thickening. No doubt yours will grow again in time."

"Indeed it won't," said Cuthie.

Tansy had looked forward to Marny's christening, but as it happened she wasn't there.

When dinner was over and everything was being made ready in the sitting-room, Hubert came to her and said, "Let's get out of this; it's all church and stuff."

Hubert was nine, up from his school in Toowoomba on holidays. She had not seen him previously but had heard it said that there was nothing else for Hubert but school. He was a pink-cheeked boy with tufts of fair hair on his head and staring, bold blue eyes with long fair lashes. he was what Granny called stout and filled his clothes to the last inch. A fine pair of scarred knees showed between his shorts and the tops of his socks.

"I've never been to church," said Tansy, looking soberly at Hubert, unsure whether she liked him or not.

"You're lucky. I go three times Sundays and to Sunday school instead of cricket. It's expected of us. I know a chap whose father is an engine driver, which I wish my dad was. But Stephen can't go on the engine with his dad as he'd like. Yet I have to go to church when I don't want to. Rummy, I think. Come on, or I'll go by myself."

Tansy was reluctant, not wishing to miss anything, but at that moment Granny called, "I hope you're looking after Hubert, Tansy," so she followed him away from the house to the paddocks lying peacefully in the spring sunshine. Land's End looked its best that afternoon, and her pride bubbled to the surface. She forgot the christening in her pleasure at showing it to someone, even a strange boy like Hubert.

However, she hardly knew what to do with him. He went instinctively towards water. She told him he mustn't but he still went. Tansy had been warned not to spoil Marny's christening with incidents. The waterhole, the dams, the trough and the dip were undoubtedly incidents.

The dip was the safest as it had very little water in it. She explained how the sheep slid down one steep side, swam the length, ordinarily full of water with disinfectant in it, and were hauled up the other; but as Hubert wanted to experiment on his own part, she steered him away from there to the sawpit tree.

"What's a sawpit tree?" Hubert asked.

"It's —" Tansy stopped, looking up into the branches above her head. How to explain about Neddy and Piebald going round and round day after day cutting the timber for the house? Or of Meredith and George — no, she wouldn't tell Hubert that.

"Why don't they chop it down? It's in the way," said Hubert.

Next they went to the graveyard. Hubert shinnied up the mulberry tree and down again but was not interested in the history of the inmates. "Why did they get buried here?"

"When there's a flood or the river is up, people die and they can't get across."

The buggyhouse suited Hubert better. It had everything in it from the dray in which the family had come from Derrick Plains to Granny's light sulky. "I say, what's all this junk kept for? Why don't they sell it and buy something else? That's what my dad did with the gig when he got the Chev. It's rather jolly, but." They climbed upon the tilted seats and whipped up imaginary horses. But this didn't satisfy him long. She took him to the large, new garage with Grand-dad's Ford standing solitary on two rows of bricks in the middle.

"Look, you could get six cars in here. And don't they know that sort of Ford has gone out? You could sell it and get a new one."

Tansy took him to the shearing shed, where the shearing was no longer done by hand but by machines. The machines looked new and shining, the smell of oil mixed with the odour of wool.

At last Hubert was impressed. "I say! Your folks well laced?"

"What?"

"They have the goods?"

"What goods?"

"Money, idiot."

"Money. We haven't any money. Wool is down and the shearers want everything these days. Everything goes back into the land."

"Same thing. I'll marry you if you like."

This gave Tansy quite a shock. Standing there in Grand-dad's woolshed, with Hubert's cold blue stare upon her, she didn't know what to say. "I'll ask Mother," she said at last.

Tansy didn't like Hubert and was tired of him. From the house the organ sounded. Hubert or no Hubert, she wasn't going to miss hymn singing. She went back to the house and left him to his own devices, which including sliding down the tin side of the dip and ripping the seat from his pants, winging a bantam with his catapult, tying knots in the cow's tails, wading into the dam and catching Grand-dad's pet perch with his bare hands.

Before this spate of mischief the crimes of Aunt Cissie's boys faded. The Rector was a mild, good man; it was agreed that Hubert was a pity for him.

What brought Tansy back to the house drove Marny from it. At the first note of the organ she gave a jump in Grand-dad's arms, where she'd been all the ceremony. He took her off for her first sight of the paddocks, coming to rest on the side of the horse trough, where he sat and looked at her till the organ was done. She was first with Grand-dad from the start, t'little lass.

With one thing and another, Marny's christening day flew over Tansy's head before she could fairly lay hands on it. It was no time from when the Chevrolet had come through the big gates, and Tansy had run up to the house after it till she shut the gates behind it and watched it disappear among the shadows, bearing the Rector and Hubert, Mother and Cuthie and Marny with it.

She returned to the house slowly. She had told Meredith that

Hubert would marry her if she liked and Meredith had laughed about it. Meredith had not laughed at her before. It had robbed Tansy of her explanation that she would rather not marry Hubert.

Far down the paddock she saw Grand-dad opening the gate through which the sheep would come to the dams for their drink in the morning.

Granny was in the kitchen. The lamp was lit and water bubbling merrily on the stove. A stiff washing-up lay ahead, all the plates and cups from Marny's christening party.

"It went off very well, I think," said Granny.

"It didn't last long," said Tansy.

"Pleasures don't. Nor sorrows either. Things come and go. Which reminds me that your visit is nearly over. We're taking you in when we go to town in two or three weeks time. I think your mother is satisfied with you. She should be. I've done my best and I must say you've turned out better than expected. I've come to find not a little pleasure in your company, but your mother and Marny need you now."

"Why?"

"Because it's good for a baby to have an older child in the house. Besides, you belong to them."

"Do I belong to the baby, too?"

"The things you ask! Of course you do. And she belongs to you. She's the only sister you'll ever have, if things go the way they should. It's good for both of you."

The words, "both of you" appealed to Tansy. She and Marny. Two of them instead of one.

By the next morning she was so imbued with the idea that Marny was someone who belonged to her that she wanted to return home straight away to claim her.

"You don't do what you want as you want it," said Granny. "It has to be thought about."

At Land's End, going to town required a great deal of thinking about. There was whether or not the sheep could do without

70

Grand-dad for the day, how the river was, the state of the weather. Grand-dad was his own weather prophet and chose the day by his own calculations. Town decided on and the morning fair, he might suddenly say, "No; not today." Sure enough a storm blew up later. On a day which hardly looked promising, he might say, "Get ready. Only good day for weeks to come." Sure enough, soon it would be fine and sunny and remain so till they were safely home again.

So Granny relied entirely on Grand-dad's judgment. Owing to all this, the necessity to go to town often disappeared while they waited. Grand-dad was relieved when this happened as he did not like the "cussed place". However, on this occasion he appeared as eager to go as Tansy herself.

"Well, I never!" said Granny as she packed Tansy's hollands and pinafores. "He wants to see the baby, no less! Now if that baby were a boy to help replace what he lost, and take over here for him when his strength goes, I could understand it. You never know what a man, at any time of life, is going to take to. But I never thought I'd see the day when your Grand-dad made a fool of himself over anything."

"It's a nice baby," Tansy pointed out. She remembered the skew-whiff bonnet, the one bright blue eye showing, and the slobbery strings in the small pink mouth.

"But when are we going?" asked Tansy, whose impatience grew as the days passed.

"Tomorrow, perhaps, if the day holds."

The back seat of the Ford was needed for the milk and eggs, vegetables, oranges, home-made bread, jams and meats that were being taken, so Tansy sat between Granny and Grand-dad in front, red feather-and-fan legs, brown buttoned boots dangling above the floor.

She took interest in the trip from under the brim of her mushroom shaped, natural straw hat. She now knew where everything was. That was Aunt Cissie's, that was Brackenridges', and there was Parkinson's out in the prairie.

The Cuthbertson house by the river was empty now, the garden already tangling. It looked sad, as grey slab houses do left to themselves. She greeted the belt of stringy-bark gums with a bounce and was told to sit still, but she knew that the sheet was now going on Aunt Jessie's line. She didn't tell Granny, having preferred it the other way herself.

Through the timber the town rose up. The sun shone on iron roofs. The streets divided it into squares, the creek cut it in halves with a silver thread. Cedar trees in blossom made a mauve haze. Far to the east, clear and blue as the eye that had peeped from Marny's bonnet, ran the line of hills.

Being now reasonably versed in letters, Tansy was able to spell out MA-LON-EYS FAM-IL-Y HOT-EL raised on a roof in large black letters.

As they passed Sprocketts' house, Aunt Jessie and Uncle Joe waved to them from the verandah. The Hogan boys were still playing marbles beside the road. They drew up in front of the Strathallan house on Palmgrove Street, and Tansy was pleased to see Dalzell Rowlands over on his gate watching her arrive home in style.

Meredith came running down the steps, a pinny over her vieux-rose crepe dress, her cheeks flushed from the wood stove. "I felt you were coming. The scones are just done," she cried.

Tansy looked at her mother, but she didn't even blush as she bent to kiss her. Tansy blushed instead.

In welcome, Grandfather bade her hop to the dunny and back, but she was too busy. She had to inspect the baby even though she was asleep. Marny was in her pram in the sheltered corner between the tank and the house. Tansy took off Marny's covers and admired her little fat knees, pink heels and small toes. She was nice, and Tansy felt gratified; she liked anyone she owned to be nice. Many had a nice smell too, and Tansy sniffed it approvingly. The baby did not stir so she left her to see that everything else was in its place.

The peppercorn still drooped by the front gate, the cedar tree was in blossom, and there was a bud on the amaryllis, waiting to burst into flower for Tansy's birthday the following week. Every year it flowered on her birthday.

But their house looked small. It had no paint. The paddock had shrunk. She wasn't pleased with the furniture either.

"Mother, are we poverty stricken?"

"Good gracious, no! We're rich. We have the most wonderful baby in the world."

"Well, are we comfortable but shabby?"

"What have you been hearing at Land's End?"

"Granny and Grand-dad don't talk much."

"That's true." She looked at Tansy, that sideways considering glance. "It must be the walls. The walls whisper out there."

7 Next morning Tansy woke to the ringing of the Angelus from the new convent across the creek. For a moment she regretted the loss of the magpies carolling in the sawpit tree, then sat up, remembering that she was home. As Marny had taken her place in the big bed in the front bedroom, she now had her own bed on the front verandah.

"Are you awake, Tansy?" came Meredith's voice from the bedroom.

Goodness me, things had changed! Meredith was up already.

"Yes, Mother."

"Well, get dressed, darling. I want you to go to Hogan's for the milk. I need it early for Marny's bottle."

Tansy was surprised. She had not been out of the front gate previously by herself. But she was also pleased, as she had always wanted to go for the milk. She dressed quickly and went to the kitchen for the billy.

"I'm to go for the milk," she told Grandfather, who was laying the fire.

Grandfather muttered something about milk and throwing

threepences away. "Thought you wasn't old enough," went on Grandfather; "you usen't to be old enough to do anything."

"I am now," said Tansy firmly. She took the billy and went.

On this first morning she ran all the way to Hogan's and, as Hogan had milked early, was back home again very quickly.

Meredith was delighted. "Granny said you were a responsible little person and so you are," she said.

Being a responsible little person made quite a change in Tansy's life. There were many delightful things which could be done from then on.

However, it didn't always happen that she returned early with the milk. She found much to interest her both ways, and Mr Hogan had erratic habits of milking. Having a number of children, the importance of Marny's bottle didn't cause him to milk earlier than he chose. Tansy often had to wait some time and on one of these occasions was married to the eldest Hogan boy before an altar of drain pipes. She gave little thought to the ceremony till it was over and one of his sisters said, "Now you're married for keeps." Tansy didn't tell Meredith owing to references to Hubert which kept cropping up. But she was uneasy, as she didn't like the Hogan boy either and for some time was of the opinion that she'd settled her own hash.

The hollands and pinafores, feather-and-fan socks and buttoned boots disappeared. Fuji silk dresses, eyeletted all over, a patent leather belt several inches above the scalloped hemline, were now being worn. It was Cuthie who provided the material and patent leather belts. She and Meredith were enthusiastic over Tansy's new appearance. Tansy, while she liked the coolness and freedom of the garments, gave no outward show of approval. They made her feel different. She was no longer old-fashioned in the way Granny liked.

Cuthie was having built for herself a small house in the paddock beside the Big House. She invited Tansy to come at any time and watch it being built. Tansy went and was delighted with the smell of new timber and the lovely, long shaving curls coming out under the plane. She took to running over every af-

ternoon and, as the children of the neighbourhood gathered
there also, made some new acquaintances. But only acquaintances. Dolores was her friend and would remain so, even if
banished forever. There was one Totty Sparrow, with whom
Cuthie wished her to be friends. But Tansy could not take to
Totty, who smelt strongly of camphor, which she wore in a little bag against her chest, held there by a piece of tape about her
neck. There was another little girl who had her name embroidered round the hem of her dress, MARY SWEET HART.
And there was a boy called Siddie, who one day drank turpen-
tine out of a bottle. Adult opinion was divided between calling
the ambulance and waiting and seeing. Waiting and seeing
won, and it turned out that he came to no harm.

Tansy was as pleasant as she could be to Totty and Mary and
Siddie and the others, but was mostly found with the carpen-
ters or sitting alone in the clover adorning herself with shaving
ringlets.

"She doesn't take to other children, Meredith," Cuthie
said. "You'd better do something about it."

"But what can I do, Cuthie?"

"Please yourself," said Cuthie. "I'm telling you, that's
all."

Several days after this conversation Meredith sent Tansy to
Chaselings' on a message. Tansy was as surprised by this as
when she was first sent for the milk. Chaselings' was over the
bridge. Meredith appeared to be worried no longer by bridges.

"I'll walk in the middle of the bridge," Tansy said, to set
any fears Meredith might have at rest.

"Goodness me! Don't do that," said Meredith, "you'll get
run over."

On the way to Chaselings' she met Dolores, who was returning home from a message.

"Why, you are a stranger!" said Dolores.

"I can't stop now, I'm in a hurry," answered Tansy.

"I'll come back with you."

A somewhat highly coloured account on Tansy's part of

Aunt Cissie's boys occupied them all the way to Chaselings'. Hubert and his behaviour more than occupied them on the way home. Still talking, they came together into Tansy's house.

"Hullo, Dolores," said Meredith, "how is your mother?"

"She's had a rather tickly cough, Mrs Strathallan. Not serious, but a nuisance. The pollen from the cedars causes it. May Tansy come over to our place?"

"Yes, if she won't be a nuisance."

"Oh, no, she's never a nuisance. We love having her."

After that Tansy went over to Rowlands' when she pleased. Things had certainly changed. She could go for the milk. She could go and watch Cuthie's house being built. She could go to Chaselings'. She could go to Rowlands'. She was free. The town was her own. She could go anywhere she liked.

No, not quite. She couldn't go to Em's.

"Remember Em?" Grandfather said to her one day soon after her return from Land's End.

Tansy thought. Yes, she remembered. "Wasn't Em the little girl who ran out to hold the bridle when George and Mother arrived at Strathlea? The one who shouldn't have."

"That's right. Living here in this town she is. In this street, too. At the other end, over the railway line. Been here a year or so, I only found out a week or two back."

"Will I see her?"

"Think not, your mother don't visit with her. I do, but."

Bent on her own pursuits, Tansy's interest in Em was less than it would have been several months before. She would have forgotten her altogether if Meredith had not said to her, "There's a woman in this town called Em. Whatever you do, don't go there. Grandfather goes there, but you must not. Em has nothing to do with you or with us."

So Meredith, Tansy saw, though fond of what she called the strict truth, didn't always tell it. There was the matter of the scones. Now Em. Em had been at Strathlea, so she must have something to do with them. Grandfather had said so anyway, that far away day when they had been sitting on the back stairs together.

"Why doesn't Mother recognise Em?" she asked him.

"Seeing you've asked a direct question, I can't tell a direct lie," he answered. "I'll put it plain and simple. Em is George's out-of-wedlock. Your mother has a dead-set on that sort of thing."

Though not as plain and simple to Tansy as it might have been, Em's connection with George satisfied her but made her regretful. "It's a pity I can't go to Em's," she said.

"You'd like it at Em's," Grandfather acknowledged.

He visited often, enjoying himself at Em's place and coming home full of unwanted news. Sometimes he bore peace offerings in unusual forms. Once it was a goat. Em kept goats instead of a cow for her milk supply.

A heated discussion took place as to who was to milk it. However, it turned out to be a Billy. Meredith suffered the smelly thing till it ate her only pair of black silk stockings, drying on the clothes-line, and took to walking up the front stairs onto the front verandah where it nibbled at the amaryllis and chewed at the ends of the lace curtains which the wind blew outwards through the sitting-room window. Then it finished off a young kurrajong tree which Meredith had been trying to grow by the front gate.

Grandfather had to take the goat back to Em's. He was sorry, as he had already started to make the cart in which he had hoped Tansy would be borne through the town behind her prancing white steed. That was Grandfather's last essay at organising a free milk supply.

Grandfather's stories of happy days at Em's among goats and babies and holy pictures made Tansy sorry indeed that Em's, like the waterhole at Land's End, was outside the homepaddocks.

The paddock behind the one in which Tansy's house sat was called Roachtown and had once had a gentleman's house on it, but this had burned down. All that was left were date palms along the one-time drive and a tank on a stand by a crumbling brick way. Tansy played there often, the date palms a source of interest, as she hoped they would put forth dates at any moment. They never did.

One day she climbed the wall, then gave a mighty heave to hoist herself to the top of the tank. But the heave had too much force behind it. She bounced across the top and down through the hole in it, which had no mosquito-catcher over it. Down into the cold, shadowed water she went to the mush at the bottom, up, down, then up. On the second trip up she collected her wits, flung up one arm and was able to grasp the rim of the hole. It took some time to hoist herself out. When at last she sprawled on top of the tank she lay trembling in the sunshine. She knew that if she hadn't been able to grasp the rim she would have been in the shadowed water forever. No one would have thought to look for her there. She decided there and then that in future she would keep clear of drowning.

She was wet and uncomfortable and had known real fear for the first time in her life. On top of this she didn't want to get *what-for* for nearly getting drowned so soon after the last time. Though Meredith had relaxed her vigilance about water, Tansy was still hearing of her last immersion. She must get fixed up before she presented herself at home.

At this crisis in her life it was Em who came into her mind as a refuge in trouble. Em, among the babies and goats and holy pictures, suddenly had an aura of warmth and comfort and uncritical kindness.

So Tansy crawled down from the tank and set out for Em's by a roundabout route.

She found Em sitting on the tankstand behind her house, enjoying the afternoon sunshine. Several small children, very red-cheeked, bulky napkins giving them a bandy-legged appearance, played in the dirt at her feet.

"Hullo," Tansy said politely. "I take it you're Em."

Em was a big woman with a broad red face. Plaits of dark, lank hair were coiled about her ears. Her breasts pulled gaps between the buttons of her blouse. The placket of her skirt was burst at the side and there was a very round mound under her skirt in front pulling it up. Her veiny, unstockinged feet were in slippers. She was doing nothing at all, which Tansy wasn't used to unless it was supported by knitting or a book.

"Hullo. Yes, Em, that's me. You're Tansy, ain't you? Have you been sent for something or just come?"

"I fell in the Roachtown tank," Tansy explained. "Mother doesn't like me getting drowned. If I went anywhere else to get fixed up they would tell her. But she doesn't talk to you so it won't get back."

"Jesus, Mary and Joseph," said Em conversationally. "Awful fusspot she always was." But she said it in a kindly way. "Real fastidious too. Keeps herself nice, I seen her once or twice since I've been here. Worn well. She doesn't look a day older than me."

This gave Tansy a shock. She fancied Em looked older than Meredith; but she remembered that Em had run out to hold the bridle as a little girl and realised she was younger.

"Babies make a mess of you and that's a fact," said Em placidly. "Keep coming too quick but what can you do about it?"

"Don't you like babies?" asked Tansy.

"Can't say I've ever thought whether I do or don't. They ain't much company at this age." She prodded the nearest one with her foot. "But a comfort in your old age, I've heard. Come on inside and we'll fix you up."

They went into the house. Tansy saw the holy pictures. There was not much else in the house but the holy pictures and more children. The floorboards were barer than in her own home, and not even stained. Tansy decided Mr Em must drink it all.

Em took off Tansy's clothes, rinsed them out and hung them on the line to dry. She lit the stove to dry out her sandals. She wiped the green sludge off her with the dishcloth and rubbed her down with the tea towel. Wrapped in this pot-marked piece of twill, Tansy waited while Em ironed her dress. It wasn't too good but good enough. Em combed her hair, twining the short, damp strands over her fingers. "You've got her hair, not his," she said. "Wished my Mother had of had curly hair."

"Marny has his," Tansy said. She didn't feel she was doing well by Em. Grandfather kept her supplied with their news and she had little to add. Besides she felt sleepy. Also she had not seen a kitchen like Em's, which was furnished, apart from the scarred table and several packing cases, with large black pots standing upon the floor. Each pot had the remains of something in it and, as the day was warm, blowflies buzzed conversationally above them.

"Fancy now. Something's got to come out somewhere."

"She's a wonderful baby, so good she wants to make you cry."

"Never had one like that," said Em.

Em gave Tansy the end off the loaf, the fresh one not the stale, with golden syrup on it, and sent her off.

She passed muster at home but for some weeks held her breath in case Em proved traitorous after all. To Em's credit she never breathed a word. So Tansy popped in on her now and again after that.

Among Tansy's other freedoms of these days was the store account.

Every time the bill came Meredith said they must never charge anything again, someone made terrible mistakes. They certainly hadn't had that much, but how could she question Mr Chaseling, when he always let them have things and didn't mind if they were late in paying? No; better to keep away from Chaselings' at the moment, wait till they had the money to pay for what they wanted. If they started clear and paid for everything, there would be no bill or the dreadful worry that went with it. You often thought you needed things which weren't really necessary. Or bought raspberry jam instead of plum. As well as being cheaper, plum went farther. As a matter of fact it stayed in the dishes and no one bothered to eat it, while raspberry disappeared as soon as it was opened.

Tansy became as good at this theoretical economy as Meredith. She could remember things they need not have had or things which had been more expensive when something else would have done.

"You can do without most things, really," said Meredith. "Why, there would not have been any Land's End now, if the old Trenworths hadn't been prepared to exist on essentials. And essentials are healthier." To bolster her confidence she would retell the pigweed and boxthorn-berry story.

For a week or so they would lead a hampered life. Everything ran out. It always seemed to be the week before Grandfather's pension. Second Thursdays, when the pension was paid, were the days government employees were paid, too. Meredith sewed for the wives of the government, but even the government employees were low at times and paid late.

Marny often rescued the situation by gobbling up all her condensed milk and arrowroot biscuits. Or Grandfather grew cranky without his Havelock Dark tobacco.

"When you come to think of it I suppose it is rather foolish to go without this week when we can pay for it next. It all evens out, I daresay. After all, an account is for that purpose. There'd be no use having one if we had money all the time. But we'll be careful."

"Oh, yes, Mother" — and Tansy would go winging off to Chaselings.

It was her soul which went winging, not her feet. The path leading to the main street was full of interest.

Once over the bridge, it started off on one side where a house had burned down. A miser had lived there and diligent people now and again found a gold piece among the ruins. Tansy felt it would be a great help at home if she found a gold piece. Her delving took the form of sitting on a charred stump

81

spending the money; it was an elastic gold piece, the one she was about to find.

On she went, past the house of the Filipino family who kept the Lily-White Wash, and the site of the Royal Hotel, which had "gone up", which was the Goombudgerie way of saying burnt down, one weekend. Next door was the wooden church, planted about with silky oaks, and the Rectory yard. At this point Tansy often crossed to the other side of the street, where the Old Glory Hotel stood on the corner opposite the church. She passed a lane called the Stock Route, along which bullock drays went now so that they wouldn't snag the traffic in the township. Here was the bakehouse, which as well as bread sold pies at Showtime or on Stock Sale Days, also buns and cinnamon loaves. These were so good and plummy they vanished before Mrs Baker's eyes something surprising as soon as they came out of the oven.

Chaselings' was just round the corner, past Tommy Low Sing's fruit shop. Now she was in the main street, with the Rose Hotel next to the Courthouse and the Crown Lands Office, in both of which the government made money sitting on their rear quarters all day with pens behind their ears. Farther along were the Pride of Queensland Hotel, the post-office, the Commercial Hotel, Grand-dad's bank and Furlong's garage, making money hand over fist, to the annoyance of the livery stables next door. In the block after that was the chemist's, which had death adders, one each in three glass bottles, blue and red and white, in the window, then the Bluebird cafe, and Victory Hotel — and along to the railway gates, the station, the Station Hotel, the sheepyards and the Yards Hotel. Beyond were several other shops and offices, as well as the premises of the local newspaper, *The Bi-Weekly Star*, and the School of Arts, where moving pictures were shown on Saturday nights, and a library was housed.

At Chaselings' Tansy was left till last to be served as it was considered she didn't mind waiting. She didn't. Time never hung heavily on her hands. She was able to go home and tell

Meredith what everyone had bought, whether they had it charged or paid. Thus they knew that the MacDougals were Catholics, as they bought a tin of herrings in tomato sauce every Friday morning; the Broughtons not as well ribbed as one supposed, Mr Chaseling having said that he could let no more out on account until the bills for the last half year were paid; the Confords lazy, buying soup in a tin instead of a penn'orth of bones from the butcher's and making it the right way with body in it. "How would one tin go round them all?" marvelled Meredith.

When the bill arrived at the end of the quarter, both Meredith and Tansy could see there were items which could have been done without. However, in the meantime, Meredith described what they purchased from Chaselings' as "the modicum, the bare essentials".

The fact was that Tansy often supplemented the modicum with something as a surprise for Meredith, who thanked her with the politeness due to the bestowal of a gift. These "gifts" took the form of tinned fish, biscuits, writing pads, ointments and headache powders. Mr Chaseling kept a varied assortment of headache powders. Meredith was never sure whether her headaches started before or after Mr Chaseling's headache powders.

Despite all the diversions Tansy had, Meredith was hard put to it keeping the child occupied. The spirit of waywardness had got into her at Land's End, was Meredith's opinion. It was all right for Granny, with time on her hands, spending all day keeping her amused, but Meredith could not.

The long Christmas holidays were particularly tedious. Dolores, tolerated by Meredith because Cuthie had pointed out that Tansy did not take to other children, was away at the seaside. Tansy wasn't content going for the milk, visiting Cuthie in her new house, taking Marny for walks, talking to Grandfather, running up to Chaselings'. (And dropping in on Em, of which Meredith knew nothing.)

"What can I do now, Mother?"

"You're to go to Cuthie's at four o'clock and see if she wants a message run."

"But what can I do *now*?"

"I don't know what you can do now, but when these holidays are over you will go to school."

Tansy was like Hubert. There was nothing for her but school.

So Tansy started school. Dolores took her. Meredith, with Marny in her arms, Grandfather, Cuthie, Aunt Jessie, Mrs Rowlands and Dalzell saw her off.

"It's the best thing for her," Mrs Rowlands said. "The improvement will surprise you."

Dolores delivered Tansy to Miss Driscoll, the head of the Infants. Miss Driscoll wore a brightly patterned floral frock. Her brown hair, streaked with grey, was in plaits coiled about her ears and a fringe fell on her forehead. She had a mole on her chin with three hairs sticking out of it.

Miss Driscoll, seated behind her desk in the classroom, opened the records book when Tansy appeared. Name, age, date of birth went into it. Year of birth was more difficult. "In the heatwave" would not do for the records. Miss Driscoll was very fond of the records, which she carried about with her.

They started the day with religious instruction. The Rector came. Miss Driscoll said, "We have Sheila with us. Is she one of yours?"

"Yes," said the Rector. "I baptised her and her sister, too."

"I couldn't make out what she was. Catholic, Methodist, or C of E."

"All the same before the Lord," smiled the Rector.

"But not for the records," retorted Miss Driscoll.

Miss Driscoll, though Tansy frequently pointed out her mistake, called her Sheila all through her Infant School days.

After eleven o'clock they had singing. Miss Harriet, who was Miss Driscoll's younger sister, though she looked just as old to Tansy, took this. She had a tuning fork which she knocked on the board and it went *ping*. Miss Harriet knocked the tuning fork quite a lot before they started singing. This was *doh* or this was *lah*, according to Miss Harriet; they both sounded like *ping* to Tansy. Then they sang several very silly little songs all together.

"Now," said Miss Harriet, "who will sing by themself?"

Tansy stood up.

"Why, the new girl. You don't appear to be shy."

"No," said Tansy; and began singing, "Don't You Remember the Time".

"Stop, stop," cried Miss Harriet. "Begin again. On the right note."

Tansy, growing annoyed, began again. She knew all the words, as Miss Harriet would find if she only let her get on with it.

"Sit down, child. Dolores, come to the front. Dolores sings it most beautifully."

"Oh, Miss Harriet," said Dolores, fixing her hair ribbon as she walked between the desks. "I'm sure Tansy meant to sing it in tune."

"Whether Pansy meant to or not, she didn't," said Miss Harriet. "There is a place we cannot mention, the road to which has paving blocks made of what people meant to do properly."

Dolores did not sing the song beautifully, to Tansy's ears. She didn't sing loudly enough and quite a number of the words were wrong. However, Tansy was distressed to find that after all her years of singing, she didn't do it the right way. She would be careful not to sing in anyone's hearing in future.

"Is that all you did?" asked Meredith when she arrived home. "One would think a great deal more could be done in a day. Miss Driscoll can't help having a mole, Tansy. It's a blemish, that's all, and she probably wouldn't look herself without it. Be thankful you haven't got one."

Tansy was.

Tansy enjoyed everything at school, but the novelty soon

wore off. While there were days when Meredith needed her kept occupied, there were other days when she considered she needed her more than the school did. Marny now spent more of her time awake. She was cutting her teeth and Meredith couldn't make headway with her sewing unless Tansy was there to take the baby to the old convent and back.

Also, if Tansy returned at lunchtime to find that the Land's End folk, or Aunt Cissie and her boys were in town, naturally she didn't go to school that afternoon.

Mrs Rowlands came over to explain that Dolores went every day, in which lay the benefit.

"But they don't do anything of importance," said Meredith.

"Oh, they take it slowly," said Mrs Rowlands, "which is best."

But it was too slow for Meredith, and what with the cold weather coming and Marny thought to be getting an eye-tooth, Tansy's schooldays lapsed for several months.

8 "We're needing more wood," said Grandfather; "I'm on the end of the last load." He paused in his chopping and leant on his axe, surveying the diminishing woodheap. The morning breeze ruffled his white beard. Puffs of grey-blue smoke went upwards from the pipe in the corner of his mouth.

"No," said Meredith as firmly as she could with two pegs in her mouth. She was hanging Marny's woollies on the line. "I can't afford another load just now. There's enough chopped to last for years."

"There is," he admitted. The woodshed was full and more was stacked under the house. "Oh well, if you want no more. But don't say I didn't leave you provided for when I go."

Tansy, who had been playing with Marny by the back steps, setting her on her feet then picking her up when she fell over, was immediately interested. She put Marny in the pram and joined Grandfather at the woodheap. Tansy had never played with dolls but treated Marny like one instead. Marny was placid, taking the erratic attentions of her sister without protest. One moment covered with kisses and hugged to within an inch of her life, the next put back in her pram and left to her own small occupations.

"What nonsense!" exclaimed Meredith. "You're not sick; you have to be sick to die."

"Don't see why," said Grandfather.

"Have you some sort of a feeling you haven't told me about, Dad?" Concern settled on Meredith's features.

"Yes, I've a feeling in my bones."

The look of concern turned to disapproval. She gave him one glance over her shoulder, rammed down the peg on the last garment, gathered up the dish which had held the washing and, without another word, turned and went inside.

"She's like my Annie," grumbled Grandfather; "can't be told nothing. Women are all alike. I'm not at all sure if men and women should marry. Don't seem to suit one another a bit."

Having delivered this speech he hoisted the axe, spat on the edge of the blade, eased the spittle along it with his thumb and continued chopping. Tansy stood by watching him respectfully. If Grandfather said he was going to die he must be. She wasn't sure what she felt about the matter. He had been there ever since she could remember. It would be strange indeed for him not to be. But she had been told so many deathbed scenes by Granny that the sight of Grandfather energetically chopping wood hardly fitted the solemnity of such occasions. Besides, the sunny winter morning, the air crisp from last night's frost, their new fowls scratching in the cover under the clothes line all gave a feeling of aliveness.

"What will happen about the pension when you go, Grandfather?" she asked conversationally.

"Buried with me," answered Grandfather. "Have to fend

for herself from now on. Which is right if she won't go and live with her husband as a woman should."

"He's not the easiest man to live with," said Tansy.

"None easier; he's never at home."

"We don't get any letters these days."

"No; she sent his letters back to him."

Tansy let the matter drop. There was no sense in the whole thing that she could see.

Grandfather finished chopping the load and stacked it away. "This axe could tell a tale or two," he said. "Funny about things like axes. Still here when you go. Ever thought of that?"

Tansy hadn't.

He took the axe and placed it where he always kept it, beside his bed. For several days he pottered about. One of these days was Marny's birthday. She was a year old. It seemed incredible to Tansy that it was a whole year since she'd been taken to Land's End with whooping-cough. Time was beginning to pass over her head the way older people complained it did. On one of these days, too, Tansy set Marny on her feet as she had been doing for months past and Marny, instead of falling over, stood there. She even took a few wobbling steps, to Tansy's and Meredith's delight.

So Marny graduated from her pram and was minded by Grandfather. He sat on the edge of the verandah and was instructed to pull her back with the crook of his stick if she tried to crawl off the rug. However, Grandfather proved a poor minder. He had never displayed the interest in Marny that he had in Tansy. Besides, Marny did not attempt to crawl away. She sat calculating on her fingers some mathematical problem of her own. It made minding an uninteresting business.

Grandfather, to amuse himself, leant over the front gate instead of sitting on the verandah. He waylaid passers by and told them in a loud voice that he was off soon.

"I've had times of one sort and another with him," said Meredith, "but nothing like this before. Why, it was the last thing he'd mention! He has never even made his last wishes known to me."

"You could ask him now," Tansy suggested.

"Indeed I won't. His conversation is depressing enough as it is. I'm trying to get it out of his head. He's quite healthy."

"He is ninety-three, which is a great age, Mother."

"Age has nothing to do with it. I could die tomorrow."

Tansy looked at her in alarm.

"But I don't intend to," Meredith said hastily.

From outside Grandfather's voice came to them, this time raised in song: "If a lady elopes down a ladder of ropes, she can go to Hong Kong for me," he carolled lustily.

They both laughed. "The best thing to do is to forget all about it," said Meredith briskly.

But this was not possible. That very afternoon he came to her and said: "I think I'll get me to the 'orspital. I don't want to be a bother here."

"So instead you want me running backwards and forwards to the hospital! That wouldn't be a bother, of course! Look here, Dad, if you're going to die you'll die here in your own bed."

"Very well," said Grandfather resignedly. "You've brought it on yourself."

He went to bed and stayed there some days. He ate heartily and slept well, read his papers and shouted the news to them through the open door. His friends called each day to see him. The house vibrated with the raised voices from Grandfather's room; it reeked of the strong tobacco which came through the door in clouds.

Meredith was baffled and annoyed and found it hard to keep the impatience out of her voice when she spoke to the old man. At the same time she followed the custom of her own family of giving the departing the food they liked best. Like all old bushmen, Grandfather enjoyed bread and meat and strong black tea. So Meredith cooked meat morning, night and noon. She cooked scones for his visitors. As she was not fond of cooking, as the butcher's bill as well as that of Mr Chaseling's was out of hand, and as she couldn't get to her sewing, the payment for which might have mended the matter, she was in an irritable frame of mind. She had decided after Marny's birth to take a resolute view of life. Her love had been foolish, she would laugh at it; she would turn her back on love, rear her two girls and allow nothing to daunt her. Now she found herself very daunted indeed. An illness that wasn't an illness, that went on day after day, week after week, with the patient sitting up enjoying himself, was simply aggravating.

Then one day Doctor John appeared at the door. "Trouble, Merry?" They had been friends since childhood. He was the only one who had ever called her that and it soothed her soul a little now. "The old gentleman's going down, I take it."

"Who told you?"

"He did. Or rather he sent a message by one of his friends. He wants to be put in the hospital so as not to die on your hands."

Doctor John went in to see Grandfather and came out laughing. "He has a feeling in his bones," he said.

"So I've heard," said Meredith grimly.

"Oh well, he's a lucky man. He's made his own decision. Not many can do that in a natural manner."

"But you don't think he's going, surely? Listen to him."

"Wouldn't like to say one way or another. Seen some funny things. And he's not exactly a spring chicken. Anyway a spell in the hospital might cure his hankering for these institutions. He's never been in one, it seems."

"Nor; nor has any Trenworth!"

"But he's not a Trenworth," Doctor John pointed out teasingly.

"Very well. He can go, but it's not my doing." Meredith's eyes grew dark with distress.

When Doctor John had gone Meredith said, "Run and find Holy Joe. If Grandfather is so keen to go the hospital he can go straight away."

Tansy fetched Holy Joe, riding back in the cab with him. But Grandfather wouldn't have Holy Joe. It had to be the ambulance.

"I've a good mind to charge sixpence for my trouble," grumbled Holy Joe as he went. "I'll think hard before I let you in my cab again, Strathallan."

"Won't be no need, Holy," Grandfather called after him cheerfully.

However, Holy Joe took Tansy to find the ambulance. She rode on the front seat beside him and came so close to falling out several times that she wondered how he had managed to keep his perch for so many years. Holy Joe took a gloomy view of the situation.

"I'd have liked to have taken him for his last ride. And I do the hospital trip regular. He could have come along with the chemist's goods, for which the chemist pays, so it'ud have cost him nothing. I daresay you're feeling pretty bad. You're losing not only a grandfather but a friend. Give him my kind remembrances if you see him alive again. I spoke hasty when we parted. When we speak hasty it's not because we don't like someone but because we're chagrined. And we get most chagrined with those we like most." Holy Joe sniffed. Tansy sniffed also.

She gave her message at the ambulance station. There was a beautiful yellow ambulance with red crosses on the side waiting beside the pavement outside. Two uniformed men got into it and purred off, leaving Tansy to walk home.

When she arrived the ambulance was outside their gate as well as Mrs Rowlands and Dalzell, Aunt Jessie, the Stones from the corner, several small Hogans and Meredith's fowls clustered about it.

Grandfather came out, unassisted apart from his stick. He had on his topcoat over his nightshirt, elastic-sided boots, and his striped woollen nightcap with the tassel like Wee-Willie-Winkie's. He handed Tansy his stick.

"You're to have it and the horseshoes. Take my papers up

to Lovey's. Don't let him give you less than a shilling for them. They're worth that and more. Buy with the shilling a token for Marny to remember me by. I've naught else to leave, but I was always a lucky man and I leave you my luck."

Lovey was a little old man who kept a fruit shop and bought newspapers by the pound for wrapping paper.

The ambulance moved off, Grandfather waving from the back. The people went away. Meredith drove the fowls through the gate, and she and Aunt Jessie went inside. Tansy followed them. Meredith wiped her forehead and sank into a chair.

"I don't know what to make of it all, Jessie," she said.

"They get funny when they get old," replied Aunt Jessie.

"Run over and tell Cuthie that your grandfather's gone to hospital, but it's not serious," Meredith told Tansy. "I don't want her to hear through someone else and think it is."

Tansy went racing through the winter afternoon to take the tidings to Cuthie.

"Grandfather's gone to hospital, but Mother says he won't die," she told her.

"Oh, won't he!" said Cuthie. "Go into one of those places and you're as good as dead." She entertained Tansy for the remainder of the afternoon with the fates of those who had entered institutions.

Meredith had to go to the hospital every evening, leaving Tansy and Marny alone. This worried her, as she was away some time and her mind had a habit of occupying itself with dangers. Suffocation, coals falling out of the stove, lamps bursting, burglars, wandering madmen. She was relieved to return the first two evenings to find her own little house still standing and the children sleeping peacefully, cuddled together in the big bed. On the third evening, however, she found the place brightly lit and Mrs Rowlands sitting in the armchair in the living room with Tansy on her knee, reading her a story.

"It was sheer luck that I heard them," said Mrs Rowlands.

"Marny is asleep again now, but I think you may have some trouble getting this one off."

"Why, what happened?" asked Meredith.

"Marny woke and cried, then Tansy woke too. She shrieked and shrieked.

"I was frightened," said Tansy complacently.

"What of, I can't make out," went on Mrs Rowlands. "Just sheer fright on its own account, no doubt. She is very highly strung."

"Oh dear," said Meredith, "that's just what I didn't want her to be."

Tansy enjoyed being highly strung and remained so on suitable occasions for some years.

In the meantime Meredith had to be beholden to Mrs Rowlands for coming over each evening to sit with the children. Neither Cuthie nor Aunt Jessie would come out on a cold night to mind a big girl like Tansy. Why, Aunt Jessie had been only four years older when she went into service.

The hospital was a mile outside the town. She could go in Holy Joe's cab, or she could go by a branch-line train which left about six o'clock, not from the station, which had a ticket office, but picking it up where it stopped for water the other side of the railway bridge. It stopped again, as if by accident, near the hospital. Meredith went by train and returned with Holy Joe.

Grandfather liked the hospital. There were people to whom he could talk, the tucker was good, they put brandy in his hot milk. The nurses were good to him. The matron was a real old battler who would have made a good help for a man settling in virgin scrub, according to Grandfather.

"He's rather spoilt," said Meredith; "I don't know how I'm going to keep it up when he comes home again."

One day when Grandfather had been at the hospital for over a week Tansy was sitting on the front gatepost enjoying the sunshine and the sound of her own low singing. She couldn't be heard from here. She saw the noon train come in, watched it pass at the other end of the street, its little black engine sending up indignant puffs of black smoke. She heard it steaming at the station, letting out great angry hisses of steam. Goombudgerie was filled with clamour at midday. Tansy enjoyed the excitement and bustle even at this distance and had strange aches and longings to go somewhere.

In the silence that followed the departure of the train she heard the unmistakable sound of Holy Joe rattling over the bridge. The cab pulled up smartly in front of the gate. Tansy jumped down from the gatepost onto the footpath. Holy Joe got down from his perch and went to the back of the cab. He hauled out a Gladstone bag and a wicker carry-all. "Follow me," he said into the back of the cab.

A tall woman came down the steps of the cab. She had large bony hands, her cheekbones and nose and chin had a covering of skin but no flesh. Her face had altogether a bare look as she had no eyelashes or eyebrows and any hair she might have was well out of sight under a large black hat. A pair of pale blue eyes looked at Tansy and through her as if she wasn't there at all. Tansy hurtled between Holy Joe and the gate, dashed through it and into the house. "Come quick, Mother! There's a woman come to stay."

Meredith hurried to the front door. "Good gracious! It's your Aunt Tessie, Grandfather's eldest daughter. I didn't think he cared for her enough to send for her."

Aunt Tessie! One of the aunts and uncles who had scattered to the four corners of the state when Strathlea went. She had been a beautiful girl with flowing gold tresses who could sit any horse on the place. Then an illness had robbed her of her hair and her ability to ride. This had turned her into a curmudgeon, according to Grandfather. Tansy had not liked the sound of the word curmudgeon, but she conceded that Aunt Tessie looked like one.

Aunt Tessie nodded to Meredith and entered the house briskly. She took off her coat and scarves and hat, which revealed faded wisps of hair barely covering a pink scalp.

"I had to come, Meredith. There's something up with Dad."

"Did he send for you?"

"He did not. I felt it in my bones."

"There's nothing the matter with him," Meredith said.

"I'll see him and satisfy myself."

"You can't. Not till tonight. He's in the hospital."

"Whatever do you mean, Meredith? In the hospital!"

"He would go there, that's all."

"Of course he would," snorted Aunt Tessie. "We all know it when our end approaches. It's given to us; a family trait. Now, who have you sent for?"

"I haven't sent for anyone. He didn't ask for anyone."

"You don't listen, more like it. You only see what's before your eyes, Meredith, and life isn't like that. Is this child old enough to send telegrams?"

"Yes," Tansy said.

"If you write out the forms," supplemented Meredith. "She won't be seven till October."

"And undersized at that."

To pour oil on troubled waters Tansy asked, "Would you like to see Marny, Aunt Tessie?"

"Who's Marny?"

"My baby sister."

"Well, Meredith, that beats everything. I come all this way at great inconvenience to myself and you're hardly civil. Then you produce an unexplained baby."

"She's quite explained," said Meredith hotly. "I'll make a cup of tea, Tessie."

"I should hope so," said Aunt Tessie severely. "I believe Em is living in Goombudgerie. Has she been let know?"

"Not by me," said Meredith. "You please yourself."

"My word, Mother. She is a holy terror," said Tansy, as Meredith stirred up the fire.

"Hush, darling. Yes, she is. But poor Tessie, one should be

lenient with her. She looks like a scarecrow and resents it as she didn't always look that way."

Tansy put her hand on the damp tendrils of hair on Meredith's forehead. "You have such pretty hair, Mother."

Meredith looked at her thoughtfully. "How odd, darling, that you should say just that."

First Tansy had to go to the post office for telegram forms. She ran there and back. Aunt Tessie filled in all the forms. Tansy sat by, excited despite herself by this drama which was being transmitted to aunts and uncles in the four corners of the state. Ravenshoe, Mount Isa, Pittsworth, Helidon, Charleville, Cunnamulla, St George, Oakey. "Come at once, Dad dying. Theresa," they said. Tansy read them on the way back to the post office. No telegram for George, she noticed. Perhaps he was in India again. Or perhaps even Aunt Tessie thought it better to draw the line. She wondered if all these people would come and, if so, where Meredith would put them. Grandfather would have enjoyed the visitors.

On the way home she called on Em. "You can come to our place if you like. Mother said to please yourself. Grandfather's in the hospital."

"Oh, the poor old gent. I'll come along with you now. Your mum won't mind a few of the kids, will she?"

"You'll have to go by yourself," said Tansy hastily. "I'm going to see Cuthie and Aunt Jessie."

"What'll I say when I get there?" asked Em, suddenly shy.

"That you felt it in your bones," said Tansy.

Before Tansy returned home, Meredith had Em walk in upon her, with three babies in a go-cart and a blue cattle-pup at her heels. However, after an hour of Tessie's unadulterated company, Em was relatively welcome. Meredith left them together and sat on the back steps nursing Marny. Jessie Sprockett's chimney puffed contentedly in the distance. Out beyond, out of sight but assuredly still there, was Land's End, where once a girl had stolen from the house at night to meet her lover under the sawpit tree. Meredith kissed the silky top of Marny's head in reverie.

Meredith did not go to the hospital that night. Aunt Tessie and Em went. "They've taken it out of my hands," Meredith said.

Aunt Tessie was away a long time. They kept the fire in the stove burning till nine then went to bed, leaving the lamp turned low on the sitting-room table.

Tansy went to sleep and half-woke when Holy Joe's cab pulled up in front of the house. She heard Aunt Tessie stamp up the stairs and into the house.

"He's gone," Aunt Tessie said briskly.

Tansy went to sleep again, but she woke first thing in the morning knowing Grandfather was dead.

It was early. Meredith and Marny and Aunt Tessie were still asleep. Tansy crept through the sitting room. In the grey light she could see Aunt Tessie's gaunt form stretched on the sofa, her bony feet sticking straight up from the covers at the bottom. In Grandfather's room she gathered up his newspapers, took them and put them in the woodcart. Taking the shafts she steered it round the side of the house and out through the gate.

There was no need to hurry; Lovey didn't open till six. There was frost on the road and she had forgotten to put on her sandals. Her feet stung and burned. She stood for some time on the side of the bridge watching the water below. It was pink from the first rays of the sun rising over the hills to the east. She stood there till the sun rose up above the hills. Then, trundling her cart, she resumed her journey along the familiar road. The bakehouse gave out the smell of yeast and new bread; at the Old Glory a man was whitewashing the front step.

Lovey, an early riser, was sprinkling the pavement when she arrived. "What does little lovey want?" he asked.

"I've brought Grandfather's papers and I won't take less than a shilling for them."

Inside the shop there was damp sawdust on the floor and she squeezed it up with her toes as he weighed the papers.

"Ninepence halfpenny," he said.

"No; a shilling."

"Tenpence."

"I must have a shilling for them; they're worth every penny of it."

"Who said they were, lovey?"

"Grandfather."

"Oh, did he? Bring him along and I'll prove they're not."

"I can't. He's dead."

"Ha! Ha! Black One-Eyed-Tom, dead! Well, so am I. I'll give you your shilling for telling a pretty story, lovey."

Tansy took her shilling and made off. She didn't like Lovey. If it had been only herself to please she would have taken the ninepence halfpenny, but she was glad she had got the best of him on Grandfather's behalf.

"Have you been for the milk, darling?" asked Meredith absently when she came into the kitchen.

"No. I took the papers up to Lovey's as Grandfather said. Here's the shilling, Mother. It's to buy something for Marny."

Meredith swung round, snatched the shilling from her and threw it up on the mantelpiece. "Sometimes I don't know what to make of you, Tansy. Thank goodness Tessie's gone to Mass and didn't hear that. Don't say another word about it.

Tansy burst into tears.

"Stop crying. It's not a crying matter."

Sorrowful, offended, Tansy went to the woodheap and sat on the chopping block where some of the nicks from Grandfather's axe still looked new. She cried heartily. At the same time she felt ashamed. She was not crying for Grandfather but for herself.

In the middle of the morning Aunt Bridie, the youngest of Grandfather's daughters, arrived from Pittsworth. "Thought I'd better come," she said cheerfully. "Can't say I ever saw much of him, but he's my father just the same."

Tansy liked Aunt Bridie, who wasn't much taller than herself but made up for it with rolls of good solid flesh. Aunt Bridie had married young and left home, and Grandfather had probably forgotten her as he had never mentioned her.

Grandfather was brought home. The black coffin with the silver handles was put in the sitting room. Tansy was lifted up to kiss his cheek. Its coldness chilled her. She felt the coldness against her mouth for many days.

In the afternoon Em came again, Aunt Jessie came, and Cuthie too. "I don't want to get mixed up in this, Meredith," said Cuthie, "but I'm here to support you."

"That's kind, but I doubt if I need supporting, Cuthie."

"You never know with this lot," returned Cuthie.

She was right. Meredith thought Tessie and Bridie had gone for a walk, but they had gone to see the priest. One only had to see Aunt Tessie storm in the front gate to know something was wrong. She came stamping into the sitting room, Aunt Bridie puffing behind her.

"Why did you turn that poor old man into a Methodist, Meredith?" Aunt Tessie demanded.

"I did not. He was born one."

"When we applied for the pension we found out."

"So you've been taking the pension all these years and not saying a word to anyone!"

"It was no secret. I hardly thought it necessary to write and tell you. It kept him and that was all."

"A pension! A Methodist!"

"I can't see," Cuthie put in, "that anything can happen but to bury him in his own plot in the cemetery which has been paid for out of his pension. Unless anyone buys another plot."

"I'm not made of money," said Aunt Tessie.

"He is a Methodist," said Meredith, "so where else could he go?"

"Strange we never heard about it before."

"If you'd seen more of him in his last years, you'd have known."

"Meredith," said Cuthie, "let the matter drop. If these people want to quarrel in the same room as the departed, let them. But don't have it on your conscience."

Everyone looked towards Grandfather lying peacefully in his coffin, his cheekbones and forehead smooth, the white beard spread on his chest. Tansy felt the strangeness then of Grandfather's not joining in the argument.

Aunt Tessie and Aunt Bridie took a long time to decide whether they would follow the funeral or not. Em made up her mind from the start.

"I'm as good a Mick as any; but I'll follow, Methodist parson and all. Good to me, the old gent was."

Tansy was very proud of Em.

The next afternoon Grandfather was laid to rest in his own plot from where the blue lines of hills could be seen and over which blew the free wind from the plain.

Meredith missed the old man and was troubled that she had paid so little heed in the last days. Tansy missed him, too; not all at once, but over the years. Marny never remembered him at all.

The Cuthbertson and Trenworth families discussed among themselves why it was a good man died hard and Black One-Eyed-Tom went easily.

"You have to suffer for your sins, somewhere," Cuthie said, which didn't make it look too good for Grandfather in the next world. But Tansy felt confident he would battle along for himself as he always had. Whether the angels were black or white wouldn't worry him. He had never drawn the colour line.

9 When the warm weather came Tansy started school again. She felt more ready for it this time.

"I hope you will be present every day now, Sheila," said

Miss Driscoll. "It is this sort of thing which makes the records look poor."

Tansy looked squarely at Miss Driscoll's mole as she replied: "Marny has the first of her teeth. We don't expect any more bother till she's cutting her two-year-olds."

"Let us hope she cuts them at night," said Miss Driscoll. "You and your mother have a lot of trouble with that baby."

"No, she's very good. It's only her teeth and the position Mother is placed in. Now Grandfather is dead we don't get the pension and she has to sew in earnest."

"Indeed!" said Miss Driscoll. "Perhaps your mother would like my custom. I hear she's a good dressmaker."

Meredith had taken over Grandfather's room as her sewing room. She had the machine under the window where the light was good and there was space for the cutting-out table. Marny sat most of the day on Grandfather's bed watching her. All would be well until she discovered that the world held interesting things for toddlers to explore. Tansy could go to school with a clear conscience.

She immediately made a new friend for herself: Miriam, a beautiful little Syrian girl. She was the only girl at the school with gold rings in her ears. Miriam was a wonderful friend. She never said a word but shot glances from her lovely eyes and smiled. She listened intently to everything Tansy said. But Meredith did not approve of this friendship, so it had to be confined to school.

Tansy became seven with the amarylis blooming and the town a mauve haze with cedar blossoms. Clouds of bees buzzed round the trees and the thick, sweet scent of the blossoms hung on the air. Goombudgerie had already entered its heatwave season in October. The days were long and summer was timeless. Christmas toys appeared in the shops and the trip to Chaselings' lengthened while Tansy stood with her two hands and nose pressed against the glass of a shop window spending on delights for Marny the gold piece she was about to dig up. Toys didn't interest her personally. When she spent the

101

gold piece on herself it went on food. Tinned peaches, pickled onions, jelly beans, bananas.

While October was rich with blossoms and long hot days and the anticipation of Christmas, another delight loomed on her horizon. The Infant School went into action for the break-up which ushered in the long vacation. There was to be a concert and prize-giving. She went home to Meredith with the news that she was to be dressed as a rose and also needed a policeman's uniform.

"On top of everything else," said Meredith.

The next day she returned with the information that Meredith was to make a sponge cake for the Member of Parliament for the District to eat at prize-giving. "Everyone's making one," Tansy said, "so I knew you'd like to as well."

"What next!" said Meredith.

Tansy felt important. As she walked Marny to the Old Convent and back she chanted:

> "Now, I'm a great big policeman,
> As anybody knows,
> I walk my beat
> Along the street
> Always on my toes."

"We're to have brass buttons down our fronts and truncheons," said Tansy. She paused to wield an imaginary truncheon, then had to haul Marny to her feet again. At any stage in proceedings Marny always sat down.

It was fortunate that the great big policeman was being chanted, allowing Tansy to be in it. There were several songs but she had declined the honour.

"No thank you, Miss Harriet."

"But why not, Pansy? I thought you liked singing."

"No, I don't."

The trouble with life is that so often joy must be given up for greater joy to take its place. Neither Tansy, her policeman's uniform, her rose costume, nor Meredith's sponge cake took part in the break-up.

Every morning she rose with the Angelus. She took the freshly scalded treacle billy, crossed Roachtown for the pleasure of being an eastern lady walking through an avenue of date palms, went to Hogans, where she left the billy to be filled, and on to Cuthie's.

Now that Meredith didn't have Grandfather to worry about, she worried about Cuthie. Tansy's visit was to make sure Cuthie hadn't died in the night. Neither Meredith nor Granny liked the idea of Cuthie living by herself, but Cuthie did and said that Meredith and Granny could both put their heads in bags as far as she was concerned. The only person she had liked to live with was her foolish old man, and now that she didn't have him she preferred it this way. Once Meredith had been able to reassure herself each morning by the sight of the smoke rising from Cuthie's chimney, but a house going up between had blocked out the view.

Cuthie was not supposed to know the reason for Tansy's inspection, but she always greeted her with, "Well, here I am," or "If I was stretched out stiff in there, what would you do?"

While always alive, there were times when she was not there, but anxiety was forestalled by the large sheet of paper tacked to her gate which could be seen from Hogan's corner. Taken home to Meredith, this would be found to say something of the nature of, "Gone to Brisbane. Feed the cat. I owe Hogan's threepence for Monday's milk. Will refund same on return. Pick up shoes left to be heeled at Tomkins'.

One morning halfway through November, Tansy went along to Cuthie's as usual. A stout double gate led into her paddock. Before the house was the newly laid out garden, a round bed on either side of the path with a small rose bush in each, Lancaster one side, York the other. The front door was open. In the sitting room was an open Gladstone bag and the two halves of a wicker carry-all. Neat piles of clothes were on the sofa and chairs.

Cuthie was in the kitchen eating her breakfast. Two chops, two eggs, tomato and bacon. Toast and marmalade and butter was also laid out neatly on the white cloth in front of her. "All's well, as you see," she said.

"Are you going somewhere, Cuthie?"

"I'm going to Sydney. I would rather have my foolish old man than go traipsing round the country. But as I haven't, it's better to go than mope around. I liked Sydney well when I saw it, which is some time ago. Mind you, if the Rector wasn't so Low I wouldn't dream of going such a long way. Low church and dull with it. His services and botheration sermons wear me out, so I don't go. At my time of life, if one hasn't a church behind one there is not much of interest to do. In Sydney I shall go to Christ Church, St Lawrence, which is Higher than even I would wish.

"I'd like to go to Sydney," said Tansy. Tansy liked to go anywhere; the mere sound of a distant name, be it Townsville, Timbuctu or Tokyo set her feet itching.

Cuthie looked at her consideringly. "Well, come along. You're quite big now and it will be good for you to find out the world isn't bounded by Land's End and this town. I am going to stay with your Aunt Ruby Buckland. She and Tom were born on Derrick Plains and married later, in town here. Poor Tom is gone now. Ruby was fast in her young days. She caught him and no mistake, though there is no issue and never was, which surprised everyone."

"Do you think Mother will let me?" asked Tansy, more interested in this aspect than in Aunt Ruby Buckland, who like Aunts Jessie and Cissie was no relation whatsoever; but to be born on Derrick Plains went hand in hand with honorary auntship.

"Why not? She was pleased to get you off her hands to that school. This will be more off her hands than that. I must send a telegram to Ruby to acquaint her of my movements. I find all the quick things these days like telegrams and telephones and pressing a button to bring on a light a great blessing. Friday. Early morning train. You'd best get home and pack.''

Tansy ran home only pausing long enough at Hogan's to pick up the milk. She felt sorry for the barefooted Hogan children who weren't going anywhere. The big policeman and curtsying like a rose were forgotten.

''Mother, I have to hurry. I'm going to Sydney with Cuthie on Friday morning's train.''

''What will you think of next?'' said Meredith. ''I'd like you to pull the paper from under the beads on Miss Raff's dress. My fingers are cramped from sitting at it so late last night.''

''We'll be staying with my Aunt Ruby Buckland,'' said Tansy.

''You're staying where you are,'' said Meredith. ''If Cuthie is going to Sydney, which I don't believe, she doesn't want you. A fine thing! Staying with Ruby Buckland, indeed!''

''But Mother —''

''Don't bother me. As if I haven't enough! I wish Cuthie wouldn't fill your head with nonsense.''

This was Tuesday. Tansy went to school crestfallen, though she told Miriam as a secret that she was going to Sydney on Friday. Miriam smiled at her dreamily.

However, when she came out of school at midday Cuthie was waiting at the big gate for her. She waved Pap's large umbrella, which she always carried, in a friendly fashion. ''Thought you'd be out about now and we can walk along together. I've sent off the telegram, you'll be pleased to know. I put 'Arriving midday Saturday. To be met. Affectionately, Caroline Cuthbertson'. She could have it by now. My! I'd like to see her face.''

''But Cuthie, I can't come. Mother doesn't believe you asked me.''

''Oh! Doesn't she?''

''No. And she doesn't believe you're going either.''

"Indeed! What would lead her to think I didn't mean what I said?"

"She says it would be a fine thing my staying with Aunt Ruby Buckland."

"Oh, is that it? Well, well! Fancy holding a grudge against Ruby still! She should know by this that Ruby was doing her a service in trying to take George off her hands. It would have been a better thing all round if Ruby had got George."

What an interesting life her mother had lived in the far away days, thought Tansy. She was pleased to find, too, that George had been in demand. She had felt that it was owing to nobody else's being willing to have him that Meredith had done so. It made the whole thing seem better and not so silly.

Up till this time Tansy had been a little in awe of Cuthie. Their acquaintanceship had grown slowly, each keeping her distance.

However, as they walked each other home that blistering November day, Pap's umbrella unfurled to shade them from the sun, the melted tar on the road burning Tansy's foot through a hole in the sole of her sandal, friendship dawned. They walked in companionable silence, each busy with her own thoughts. Tansy felt Cuthie would have her own way with Meredith. Cuthie always had her own way.

"Now you keep quiet," Cuthie warned as they went in the gate. "Let me handle it."

Tansy was only too willing to do so.

Inside, the house was like a cool cavern. Whatever breeze there was blew from front to back through the open doors. The sparse furniture, the few covers, the stained floors all made for coolness. Now Grandfather had gone the fire no longer blazed in the stove all day. Meredith cooked the midday meal on a primus. Its zinging and the buzzing of a blowfly against a window pane sounded through the house. The smell of methylated spirits accompanied that of potatoes boiling.

Cuthie launched on her subject immediately. "You've heard that Tansy and I are going to Sydney, Meredith."

"I heard but I certainly didn't believe it."

"Why not? What harm in going to Sydney?"

"And staying with Ruby Buckland?"

"In a way she owes it to you."

"She owes me nothing."

"Anyway," said Cuthie briskly, "that's a red herring. What I think is that you want a holiday yourself. You've been working too hard. Take the baby and go to Land's End while we're away."

"I can't do that," protested Meredith. "There's all the dresses I've promised."

"Unpromise them," said Cuthie. "If you took ill you couldn't do them. And you will, if you keep on this way."

This was strange from Cuthie, who disliked anyone being ill, and pooh-poohed Meredith when she complained of a pain here, an ache there. Tansy gazed at Cuthie with respect. She would never have thought of going about the matter in this manner.

"I am at the end of my tether," admitted Meredith. "Dad's death coming so suddenly, then everything on top of it." Suddenly she became wary. "But I don't see what that's got to do with Tansy going to Sydney," she said. "She can come out to Land's End."

"No sea there," said Cuthie promptly. "A child needs sea air once in a while."

"There is that," said Meredith, "and she hasn't seen the sea. But then there's the fare."

"I'll pay it," said Cuthie.

"You can't afford to do that. You'll need your money to see you out."

"Not me," said Cuthie, "I have it arranged. If I outlive what I have I'll sell the big house."

"Sell the house!" cried Meredith, shocked. Cuthbertsons and Trenworths had a firm habit of keeping what they had.

"Can't eat it as it stands. And if I outlive that I can get the pension. If they gave it to Black One-Eyed-Tom, they'll give it to me."

"Oh, Cuthie! What would Mother say?"

"Catherine can put her head in a bag," stated Cuthie. "Now I take it everything's fixed for Friday morning."

"Oh, no. I couldn't get Tansy's clothes ready in time."

"What she's got will do. She doesn't wear much."

"Tansy," said Meredith, "off to school or you'll be late. Coming home get six yards of washing elastic at Chaselings'. You can't go to Sydney with your pants falling off."

Tansy was full of joy in the intervening days. She hugged Marny almost to death, patted Meredith approvingly every time she was near her, kept looking at the clock when she was home in the hope of hurrying the hours along.

"You don't seem able to get away from me fast enough," said Meredith reproachfully.

"You've got Marny," said Tansy, "and you'll have Granny and Grand-dad and the Sawpit Tree."

"I'm not as fond of the Sawpit Tree as you are," Meredith pointed out.

Tansy had one regret. It occurred to her that at the break-up she might have taken a prize. As Cuthie was so approachable these days she told her about it.

"A school prize!" exclaimed Cuthie. "Why, they're hardly worth having. Totty Sparrow has had *Eric, or Little by Little* three years running. Why do you want a prize?"

"I haven't a book of my own."

"Didn't I give you *Brer Rabbit* last Christmas?"

"No. You must have given it to someone else."

"Oh, very well." Cuthie reached down a tin from the mantel above the stove and counted out two and ninepence. "Go up to the paper shop and buy *Seven Little Australians*, by Ethel Turner."

Tansy still wasn't quite satisfied. "The prizes are written in," she said.

"I'll write in it," replied Cuthie sturdily. Write in it she did:

"To Tansy from her own Cuthie. On the eve of departure for Sydney where she is going to live with her Aunt Ruby Buckland, hard by where the Seven Little Australians lived."

Tansy went to school in the morning the day before they left. She told Miss Driscoll that she was going to Sydney.

"What nonsense!" said Miss Driscoll. "Why would you go to Sydney? You must bend in the middle to curtsy like a rose, Sheila!"

She was not at school that afternoon. She was being bathed and packed up. In future, when girls said they were going to Sydney, Miss Driscoll would believe them.

The main pieces of luggage, some labelled "Cuthbertson" and some "Strathallan", were taken to the station late on Thursday afternoon in the cart owned by Mr Perce Loveday, the husband of Uncle Joe Sprockett's niece.

Tansy alternated between being crimson in the face and deathly pale with excitement. She slept little on the Thursday night.

"I need my brains brushed letting Cuthie get away with this," said Meredith.

Tansy didn't think so.

In the early hours of Friday morning Tansy rose and dressed. Meredith was already up, not having been to bed, it appeared. But despite the earliness of rising, Tansy was barely ready in time. Cuthie made her appearance before they finished breakfast. She carried a large cloth bag, Pap's umbrella, a little white wicker bag with the sandwiches and several bundles of plants.

"Cuthie, it's not three," protested Meredith.

"The train is due to leave at four and there's much I have to see the stationmaster about first, travelling alone as I am with a young child."

Tansy kissed Meredith and the sleeping Marny and off they set. Cuthie had no use for Holy Joe's cab. She considered her

109

own legs good enough. When they gave out she intended to hire a car from the garage; their best car at that.

They took their time through the grey and silent town, talking of the things they were leaving, the delights ahead.

"Grand-dad's woolstore burned down in Sydney a few days ago," said Cuthie. "Still smouldering, they say. We might see it and be able to tell him all about it when we come home. He's a hard man to have a conversation with. Nothing seems to interest him. But that should."

Tansy agreed. Though he wouldn't say much, Grand-dad would no doubt be delighted to know they had seen the place where his wool had disappeared. The clip of the season, too.

"According to your Aunt Ruby Buckland," went on Cuthie, "we have to ride in a ferry to get to her place. From the ferry as one leaves the quay one can see a bottle outlined in electric lights which pours wine into a glass in lights, too. She said so, anyway. Whether it's still there I don't know. Ruby is not the best correspondent."

The station was in darkness when they arrived. "Best rest our haunches," said Cuthie, and they sat down until the stationmaster appeared. He did not have much time for Cuthie then. The train was due, lamps had to be lit, a crate of fowls to be let off at Helidon found and given attention.

Carts and cabs rattled up outside. Mr Perce Loveday and Holy Joe came onto the platform. Holy Joe looked at them reproachfully. "Made the trip by myself," he said. "Many have now grown too flash to ride the way their forbears rode."

"When times change, change with them. Buy a car, Holy Joe," said Cuthie.

Holy Joe strode off and left them.

When the first bustle was over, the stationmaster devoted himself to Cuthie. They stood talking on the edge of the platform, looking into the west, the stationmaster now and again jumping onto the line and putting his ear to the rail till at last he shouted, "She's coming."

The train was crowded. Out west the large sheds had closed

and the shearers were heading south with their cheques to go "on the bust". They were in a holiday frame of mind. The occupants of an already full carriage made room for Cuthie, and Tansy was placed upon the knee of a red-bearded giant who was playing a mouth organ. He went on playing and, apart from providing a seat, took no notice of her. She now knew how insignificant a wagtail felt, perched on a cow's back.

The train started but stopped shortly afterwards to take on water. They started again but halted once more to let a pig train pass. Next time they started the train was in motion for five minutes before it panted to a standstill.

"Bags from the silo," explained a shearer.

The train started but went backwards. Milk cans at a siding had been forgotten.

"We'll get to Darwin, not Sydney, at this rate," Cuthie said impatiently.

The milk cans recovered, the train went forward at a smart pace. Just as the movement began to feel like perpetual motion, it stopped so suddenly they were all thrown together. Tansy's head hit the mouth organ and the mouth organ hit its owner's teeth. He swore and went on playing.

"Now what is it?" demanded Cuthie.

The shearer nearest the open window on the right-hand side put his head through it. "Nothing this side. Hey, Bill, shove yer head out that side and see if there's anything."

Bill obliged. "Only a woman with a kid on one arm, handing up a note to the engine-driver."

"So you see, Missus," said another shearer, "it's just someone who wants a little bit of this and that brought up from Toowoomba for her."

"What a way to run a train service." exclaimed Cuthie.

On they went and kept going till they arrived at a small town. The train stopped. The shearers tumbled out onto the platform. Cuthie and Tansy sat in the empty carriage. Then a friendly guard put his head through the window, "You oughter stretch your legs and take a cuppa. We'll be here a bit."

"Not too long, I hope," said Cuthie severely. "We're connecting with the Sydney Mail in Toowoomba."

The guard shook his head. "Should do, but it don't always come about. Ought to connect with the Sydney Mail, barring accidents."

There were no accidents, so they connected with the Sydney Mail. Only just; but that was good enough, Cuthie pointed out, having learnt patience on the way.

When they were in this train Tansy asked, "Are we coming up to Sydney now, Cuthie?"

"No, not yet. Don't ask again till tomorrow."

Tomorrow seemed a long way off. Tansy began to wonder why Cuthie had insisted on bringing her all this long way. Cuthie had been wondering the same thing for some hours past.

10 They were met at Sydney Central by Aunt Ruby Buckland, who burst on Tansy's vision as a mass of pink crepe-de-Chine with white laced shoes, flesh silk stockings and a leghorn hat with a large rose weighing down the floppy brim. With the pinkness of the rose, the dress, and Aunt Ruby's cheeks and chin and nose, she made a colourful blur among the hurrying, more soberly clad travellers. While her face and cheeks were plump, her nose and chin were sharp and so close together there was just enough space for her ruby-red outjutting mouth. Coils of yellow hair could be seen under her hat, but her eyebrows and eyelashes were white. Attached to her well curved body were spindly arms and legs. Tansy's first impression of Aunt Ruby was that she hadn't been put together very well.

"This is a surprise, Aunt Caroline," said Aunt Ruby as she helped Cuthie from the carriage. "It astounded me to find you were still alive, let alone fit to come this distance. But you are most welcome.''

"Thank you, Ruby," said Cuthie. "I'm quite fit, though blown out a little by the journey. You keep up your dress, I see."

"More and more since poor Tom went. I need interest."

"Didn't you wear mourning?"

"Yes, for the allotted time and not a day over. Tom wouldn't have wanted it. And pink brings out the best in me."

"I'll admit you've worn well," said Cuthie.

Aunt Ruby tossed her head so that the rose flopped. "There's no reason why I shouldn't wear well, Aunt Caroline." Her pale blue eyes behind rimless spectacles came to rest on Tansy, who was keeping as close to Cuthie as she could. "Run off, dear. This nice lady doesn't want your sticky hands all over her."

"That's all right, Ruby," said Cuthie absently, more interested in finding her cloth bag, "she's been all over me all the way down. I brought her."

"You *brought* her? Good gracious, Aunt Caroline! How are we to get around with a child of this age? Who is she?"

"My great-granddaughter, Tansy Strathallan."

"Don't tell me!" exclaimed Aunt Ruby. "I had no idea there was issue." She looked critically at Tansy, who scowled back, not pleased at being called "issue". "I'd forgotten the old days, Aunt Caroline, but they're sweeping back over me."

"Where do we go now?" asked Cuthie.

"To the tram. Follow me."

They followed Aunt Ruby's stiffly corseted pink crepe-de-chine figure. Everything was hurry and bustle. Tansy had never seen so many people or heard so much noise. The din of the noonday train at Goombudgerie faded before this conglomeration of sound. Never before had she faced the possibility of being trampled underfoot or run down by trolleys, the knowledge that if she stopped clutching Cuthie's skirt she would be whirled into the crowd and lost forever.

With their hand luggage they boarded the tram and were bumped and bounced down Castlereagh Street. There were tall buildings and shop windows decorated for Christmas.

The tram stopped at the quay and they alighted. For the first time Tansy smelt the salt smell of the sea, and mingled with it another familiar smell, a smell which overcame her with a yearning for Land's End.

"A woolshed, Cuthie; someone has a woolshed?"

"A woolstore, dear," said Aunt Ruby. "Wool's kept there till it's sold and sent overseas."

Cuthie was too occupied to be bothered about woolsheds or woolstores and Tansy's wave of homesickness was dispelled by the sight of the ferry, the clatter of gangplanks and her first embarkation. They sat outside and saw the bottle and wineglass. "It's not lit up now," said Aunt Ruby, "that's only at night."

The ferry moved smoothly over the blue water, drew in twice to small wharves, then all too soon stopped at the wharf Aunt Ruby said was hers. Another tram waited; they climbed aboard and it started immediately with a great clang and clatter and a series of jumps and bounces which outrivalled riding on the front seat of Holy Joe's cab. The tramline wound upwards, large houses with smooth green lawns on either side. Against the brick walls of the houses large blue flowers bloomed on dark green bushes.

"Hydrangeas," said Cuthie.

"Hydrangeas!" exclaimed Tansy. "Is this Cornwall, Cuthie?"

"No, of course it isn't. It's New South Wales."

"Oh! We're across the MacIntyre."

"What a little bushwhacker it is," laughed Aunt Ruby.

Bushwhacker! Tansy didn't like the sound of that. "What's a bushwhacker?"

"It means down from the bush," said Aunt Ruby.

"But I'm not. The bush is out beyond."

Aunt Ruby looked over Tansy's head at Cuthie. "I take it, it's a bit of a caution, Aunt Caroline?"

"They don't come more so," said Cuthie, smiling. Tansy didn't know what a "caution" was, but as it seemed to please them she didn't mind being one. She began to take to her Aunt Ruby Buckland. The tram stopped.

"What do we do now?" asked Cuthie, who was finding this continual changing of conveyances wearisome.

"We have a twenty minute walk," replied Aunt Ruby cheerfully.

"I must say you live a long way from anywhere."

"Not at all. I find it most convenient. When what poor Tom left matures I will buy my own house in this same suburb." They crossed a road with more tramlines; these were the main lines, Aunt Ruby said. "Now Tansy," she went on, "as you're no doubt old enough to run messages, this is our butcher here on the corner. The grocer's is farther down, and along there is the draper's where we get what we forget in town. They are all on our side. On no account must you cross this road. What with the trams hardly a day passes without a child getting skittled. It turns my stomach when I hear about it."

Tansy promised not to turn Aunt Ruby's stomach.

They turned into a tree-lined street, at the end of which a patch of blue water could be seen with a little boat rocking on it. "There's the harbour. See you don't fall into that. Full of sharks. Our neighbour's dog went the other day. Splashed in and wasn't seen again."

They had walked almost the length of the street when Aunt Ruby turned in at the gate of a semi-detached cottage. There was a privet hedge, a small square of lawn, a red-tiled verandah with a gas-box at one end. It looked strange to Tansy. They entered through the front door into a narrow hall where the gas had to be lit, though it was early afternoon on a bright summer's day. People could be heard plainly on the other side of the wall.

"Good heavens, Ruby!" exclaimed Cuthie. "I didn't know you were living like this."

"Like what?" asked Aunt Ruby.

Tansy, while disappointed with Aunt Ruby's house, enjoyed the mystery of its darkness, the many smells which circulated through it. Floor polish and mothballs, gas fumes, stale flowers in a vase, fish fat, peaches and bananas. There was an airless breathlessness which went to her head.

"Aunt Caroline, it looks as if that child is passing out on her feet."

"Thank the Lord," said Cuthie. "I knew it must happen sometime."

Tansy was put to bed with her clothes on in the double bed prepared for Cuthie. "It's fortunate I kept it when I got the new one," said Aunt Ruby. "I kept it for sentiment's sake, poor Tom dying in it."

Later, as if from far away, Tansy heard both their voices talking about picking up the luggage. "We'll both have to go to carry it," said Aunt Ruby.

"But how can I go and leave her alone in the house?" asked Cuthie.

"She won't come to any harm. If she does Meredith has the other one," said Aunt Ruby comfortably. "Besides, she can always go north."

"An odd way to look at it," said Cuthie.

Once they became used to the narrow dark house, Tansy and Cuthie found it pleasant enough at Aunt Ruby's. Aunt Ruby herself saw nothing wrong with her house, so Cuthie's first unwitting remark went over her head. Indeed, Aunt Ruby felt they would find it a welcome change after the weatherboard houses of Goombudgerie. This house was of brick, with a tiled roof; bricks and tiles were commodities on which Aunt Ruby set great store. The leaning backyard fence was covered with choko vines which looked green and pleasant. Gum trees grew in a gully behind. Cicadas chanted and clacked and rattled all day long.

Aunt Ruby lived a busy life among her neighbours, running in and out of their houses or having them run into hers. In the semi-detached which adjoined were the Moneypennys, a youngish married couple with five children. Across the road were a man and his wife who weren't married, according to Aunt Ruby, though they looked married to Tansy. This necessitated the wife's coming over often to seek advice from Aunt Ruby, or drawing Aunt Ruby over there to offer advice. Between times Aunt Ruby told Cuthie about it.

"No good ever comes of irregularity, Ruby," said Cuthie.

"They're most devoted," replied Aunt Ruby. "It's just that she has no rights."

"How could she expect any?" asked Cuthie.

Tansy had the feeling of growing up overnight. Breaths of other lives blew upon her, the sun shone as it had at Land's End and Goombudgerie, but on a wider, more shifting scene. People intertwined themselves with her days, the cicadas clacked, the tarry road of the street ended in rocks where children could scramble and the rocks fell to the sea beyond. The sea gave off a heady, briny smell which spilled over the days and made the nights balmy. At night, lights twinkled and the stars were high and pale and far away. This was Sydney and Tansy, devoted as she was to Goombudgerie, gave it a small portion of her heart there and then.

For the first few afternoons she played by herself among the rocks. Cuthie and Aunt Ruby sat on a seat not far away, busy with their talk of olden times. There were other children there but Tansy had always been happy playing by herself. One afternoon, however, she climbed the highest rock and as her head came above it, another head appeared at the other side. She recognised them as belonging to the eldest Moneypenny girl. Her name was Cassandra.

"Hullo," said Tansy.

"Hullo," said Cassandra.

They scrambled simultaneously onto the rock and sat side by side in the late afternoon sunshine. They were about the same age and the same size, bare brown legs and arms, short print dresses. The sea breeze lifted Tansy's rough brown curls, ruffled the smooth, silky blackness of Cassie's square-cut bob. Cassie had a cowlick which made a peak in the middle of her forehead; her chin was pointed. She had an elfin look which Tansy liked. They didn't say anything further. At last they scrambled down the same side of the rock together, linked arms and wandered homeward.

Aunt Ruby had already suggested to Tansy that Cassie would make a good friend for her. Mrs Moneypenny had pointed out to Cassie that Mrs Buckland had a young visitor who would make a companion for her through the school vacation. But neither Tansy Strathallan nor Cassandra Moneypenny were the sort of girls who accepted friends foisted on them by someone else. They chose their for themselves.

"Well, what do you think of that?" asked Aunt Ruby.

Thereafter, being wholehearted in matters of friendship, Tansy was more likely to be found at Moneypenny's than Buckland's.

Besides the tram and ferry rides, lunch in the gardens and long golden afternoons spent playing with Cassie, there was the zoo, near at hand, to visit, and there was also a beach. On Cassie's birthday the Moneypennys went for a picnic to the beach. Tansy, well established as Cassie's best friend, was taken along too. She looked forward eagerly to splashing in the water but found to her own dismay that she did not like it. It was unexpectedly cold, the waves tumbled her about and the salt water filled her mouth and ears and eyes. Half an hour later, her skin exposed for the first time to sunlight, she was already sore. She tried to oblige Cassie by pretending to like the picnic but was shivery and miserable. There was no need for anyone to tell Tansy again to keep away from water.

Tansy never found out where the Seven Little Australians

lived. Her book had been left behind in Goombudgerie by mistake. However, she saw where Barcroft Boake, who had written a poem called "Where The Dead Men Lie", had hanged himself and where he had been buried. She and Cuthie walked across the gullies one hot day to view these things. The exact spot of hanging could not be identified. It was said to be "near the big pipe". But when Mr Boake had chosen this place for his end it was not the sewerage farm and there were now many big pipes. However, they found his grave in the unhallowed part of an old cemetery and Cuthie pulled up enough weeds to plant a sprig of rosemary she had picked over a garden fence on the way.

Tansy stood in the hot sunshine, looked at the rosemary, thought of Aunt Cissie and her boys and cried.

Cuthie did not like tears. "Stop that. There's no need for it. His troubles are over."

"Did he have a lot of troubles, Cuthie?"

"He was a poet and they are not happy without them. Best to keep away from that sort of thing. Shakespeare lost his only son, you know."

They bought apples at a little shop near the cemetery and ate them on the way home, Cuthie still having every one of her own teeth, of which she was proud. When they arrived home Aunt Ruby had gone to town and they had no key. Tansy had to scale a drainpipe near the open bathroom window, facing death by dizzy heights. She found it easy; but Cuthie was astonished by her performance, so Tansy allowed herself full glory.

"You should have seen her," Cuthie told Aunt Ruby later. "She'd get through a keyhole."

"How did you come?" asked Aunt Ruby.

"By the gullies."

"You shouldn't have done that. The blackberry bushes are full of snakes this time of the year."

Tansy found the city more full of dangers than Goombudgerie had been. Sharks in the water, traffic running wild on roadways, strange men not to be spoken to, snakes in blackberry bushes, ticks on tickbushes.

Cuthie and Aunt Ruby got on well together. Though they were different sorts of people and saw eye to eye on nothing, they were both willing to live and let live. They said so often. They talked a great deal of the olden days. Tansy heard much of poor Tom and would have heard a lot about George, except that when they started on him, they sent her off to play with Cassie.

Cuthie said in private that Aunt Ruby was a slap-dash creature, but she did one good — she blew the cobwebs away. Tansy found Aunt Ruby's slap-dashedness much to her liking. It made for meals with very little washing-up and excused Tansy from house-cleaning activities. These were rare anyway, it being Aunt Ruby's opinion that all was well if left alone. Besides, Aunt Ruby needed all her time to keep herself spruced up.

Aunt Ruby lived a comfortable, carefree life, Tansy felt. Her only sufferings had to do with tight corsets and shoes that pinched. She forestalled any ailment that might be about to overtake her with a glass of port. She confessed to having no nerves whatsoever.

"Which is a blessing," said Cuthie. "It prevents rubbing them the wrong way."

Christmas came and went. Their stay with Aunt Ruby had a permanent feeling.

"Any time you'd like us to move off, Ruby, just say so," said Cuthie.

"No hurry, Aunt Caroline. You don't have anything to go back for."

"Only school when it starts."

"Oh! If it comes to that Tansy can always run along to school with Cassie."

However, about the middle of January, Cuthie's conversation turned from the delights of Sydney, to her own little house. She would interrupt Aunt Ruby in the middle of a sentence to say, "I wonder if Lancaster and York survived the summer," or, "those zinnias I planted should be flowering."

To Tansy, Cuthie spoke of her statue of Queen Victoria on the sideboard, the teak box with the inlaid mother-of-pearl which had been her own mother's tea chest, her little organ on which she played hymns for herself. In the eyes of both of them these things became valuable.

Tansy began to want her mother and Marny. According to a letter from Meredith, Marny was a real little girl now. Out at Land's End she had loved the Sawpit Tree, dancing under it and clapping her hands. Grand-dad had given it to her. "It's yours, t'little lass, for what use you can make of it." This upset Tansy. The Sawpit Tree was hers. She saw it first, as Dolores would have said.

Though Aunt Ruby was as kind as ever and Sydney as beautiful, it began to fade before their eyes. They grew miserable. As Cuthie could bear anything but misery, something had to be done.

"We're homesick, that's a fact," said Cuthie. "It's a pity, but there it is. Nothing to do but pack ourselves up."

She began packing, much to the surprise of Aunt Ruby. "But when are you going, Aunt Caroline?"

"Tomorrow," said Cuthie. "When I go, I go."

So goodbye to Sydney of the tall buildings, the bouncing trams, the ferries plying backwards and forwards across the blue water, the houses of dark bricks and red tiles — Sydney, old but still young, with gullies where the gum trees grew; goodbye to Cassie of the blue eyes, the pointed chin and the dark peak on her forehead where the cowlick swept her fringe back; goodbye to Aunt Ruby in her pink crepe de Chine dress, white laced shoes, flesh silk stockings and leghorn hat, a pleasant blur of colour among the soberly dressed people on the platform waving the train away.

They were off to surprise Meredith and Marny and Aunt Jessie with their quick return.

Meredith and Aunt Jessie weren't as surprised as all that. They had been wondering for some weeks what was keeping them.

For the sake of politeness, Meredith wrote to Ruby Buckland and thanked her for having Tansy. Equally polite, Aunt Ruby replied. After that, the correspondence was kept up.

Tansy was pleased. She looked forward to the rare letters from her Aunt Ruby Buckland. Each one reawakened in her mind the glimpse of magic she had had till memory, willing to be duped, turned it into a fairytale.

11 Much had changed in Goombudgerie during Tansy's absence. The Old Glory had burned down. On one of the old burnt-out blocks a row of shops had been started. The wooden church had been swung round into another position in the churchyard and was being turned into the Parish Hall. The foundation stone of the new church had been laid by the Archbishop.

As to the Strathallans themselves, Meredith having been at Land's End and not yet having caught up with her sewing, they were very poor. Poverty is always dashing after a fine holiday.

For Tansy there was a big change. The morning when she had told Miss Driscoll that she was going to Sydney had been her farewell to the Infant School, Miss Driscoll, Miss Harriet and her tuning fork. Dolores and Tansy went into the Big School together, into the same class.

Meredith had not thought a great deal of Infant School, disappointed by its poor standard of teaching. Now she was pleased things were starting in earnest at last. On the other hand the school required more than she thought possible. Except for Mr Chaseling and his willingness to oblige with rulers, rubbers, pencils, notebooks and the First Red Reader, Meredith would have had to tell Miss Driscoll regretfully that Tansy must stay down for another year. In the interval Dolores would have gone ahead of Tansy and Meredith would not have liked that. She was glad Tansy was smarter than Dolores, able to do the uninteresting part of school in less time. This would prove to Mrs Rowlands that there was no need for her to take it upon herself to explain to Meredith what Tansy should do and what she shouldn't.

As well as so much stationery, the school needed a piece of fine white madapollam for Tansy to make a petticoat. Meredith was outraged by this. She could make Tansy's petticoats if she needed them; as it was Tansy did not wear them. Meredith hated petticoats — in her day children were smothered in the wretched things.

There was no danger of Tansy's being smothered in her petticoat, however. It never got beyond one side gathered in and what was supposed to be a run-and-fell seam. In time the fine white took on a grey limpness, ink from the ink-well which had a habit of jumping out of its hole in the desk and upsetting on sewing days and blood from Tansy's pricked fingers. The garment soon resembled the dishcloth Em had washed Tansy with on the day she had fallen in the Roachtown tank.

Meredith, Cuthie and Aunt Jessie all took keen interest in this higher form of scholarship upon which Tansy was launched. They wished that they had had the same chance. Meredith had been taught her twice-times and letters by Granny, and she had picked up reading from the *Bulletin* while she stitched its pages together each week so it wouldn't fall apart in Grand-dad's hands. She had boarded for several years at the old convent; but all she got there were the corns she still had, Sister not allowing her to change her new shoes, which pinched.

Aunt Jessie could not recall anyone teaching her anything. What she knew had come upon her from time to time.

Cuthie had spent many years in the schoolroom at home in England, but in those days boys received the best end of the stick. Her schoolroom experiences had more to do with sago pudding, bread and butter, muffins toasted in front of the fire and a rocking horse than lessons. Then she met Pap, a fugitive in London from the famine in the north, and decided to risk the future in the colony with him. Cuthie had set out for the colony in the same hasty manner she now set out for Sydney, Brisbane or Land's End. "When I'm going, I go."

Tansy enjoyed being modest as she told the delighted Cuthie of her success in her new way of life. Cuthie often sat down there and then to write off to Aunt Ruby or Granny about it.

Tansy sometimes met Aunt Jessie on the bridge when she was coming home from school. Aunt Jessie in her violet print, black shoes and stockings, parasol upraised, big square basket over her arm, off for her messages in the cool of the afternoon. Aunt Jessie spent her life in a hurry, but she could always spare time to shoot questions at Tansy which Tansy answered like anything. "You can't daunt her in answering up," Aunt Jessie told Meredith. Tansy found this very heartening.

When Tansy arrived home, Meredith would be bent over the machine, pedalling away, singing, "I am the honeysuckle, you are the bee", or, "The saucy little bird in Nelly's hat". She had taken to singing to keep herself cheerful. Marny sat on Grandfather's bed playing with empty cotton reels lined up on the end of the machine like the children at Tansy's school.

"How did you get on today, darling?"

"Oh, it was good. I was called out to read in front of the class." Tansy read better than anyone else, much faster and louder. She knew *Lost* all through, while the others knew only the first verse. She did her sums the quickest and had time on her hands while the others were finishing, and didn't think it would interest Meredith to hear of the crosses which decorated her exercise. Her hand was up first in mental arithmetic. Miss Peacebody's "Put your hand down and think, child" would scarcely interest Meredith either. Compositions were no bother, though Miss Peacebody tried to hold her back by wanting her only to use words of which she knew the meaning.

"How foolish," said Meredith. "How can you learn anything if you use only what you know?"

Tansy was glad Meredith agreed with her on this point. No Latin as yet, unless it had been on the days she was away or the week spent at Land's End. She didn't really like dictation but it was easy. They read out of a book and you wrote it down.

Early in the Big School days Dolores arrived one afternoon with her exercise and Red Reader.

"Now, what is it you want, Dolores?" asked Meredith.

"I've come so that Tansy and I can do our homework together."

"What's homework?"

"It's what you do in the day gone over so you'll remember. Or preparing new work for tomorrow."

"How silly! After being cooped up all day coming at it again. Tansy takes her sister for a walk in the fresh air, much better for her. She doesn't have to do homework, she's rather ahead."

In time they had the exam. Tansy enjoyed the exam, all the importance, the sharpened pencils, the margin on the side of the exercise for marks, all books under the desk so you couldn't cheat, the Headmaster himself taking an interest in lower third, walking between desks, his cane in his hands clasped behind his back, peering over their shoulders to see what they were doing.

Tansy's knowledge of the Headmaster had been limited to fall-in, in the playground, when he walked between the lines, swinging at bare legs with his cane as if by accident. Her legs had an inevitable way of being in the wrong place.

After the exam came the report. She took it home, delightedly, reading it on the way.

CONDUCT	ATTENDANCE:
fair	*irregular*
Marks obtained	Maximum marks

	Marks obtained	Maximum marks
Sums	10	50

Reading	6	10
Poetry	7	10
Dictation	0	10
Composition	5	10
Sewing	2	10

Number in class 24   Place in class 24

General Remarks: Obedient and obliging, but will talk in class, so conduct can only be termed fair. Misses too many half-days. Would like her present all day in future. [Impossible. Aunt Cissie and her boys came in often and the Land's End folk more than they had previously, Grand-dad liking to see t'little lass every month or two.] Feel she could do better with concentration. A firmer hand at home might be helpful. [Ah yes, indeed, but according to the letters Meredith steamed open, then stuck down carefully before returning, that firm hand was either escorting horses between Darwin and Bombay, opening a new mine in the vicinity of Mount Isa, or eating pigweed in the Gulf Country, owing to being lost for many days without tucker or water.]

When Tansy came home she found Aunt Jessie there, sitting on Grandfather's bed beside Marny. "Read this, Mother. It's from school. You have to sign it and send it back."

Meredith took it. "Ah, the report," she said, and she and Jessie smiled at one another. She read it. She read it several times. The smile faded from her face, her mouth grew thin and her forehead puckered.

"I don't understand this, Tansy. I don't understand it at all. It says number in class, twenty-four. Place in class, twenty-fourth."

"Yes, that's where I am."

"But that's bottom."

"It's where you see the blackboard best."

"Good Lord! Don't say you have my eyes!"

"Let me see," said Aunt Jessie. She looked for a long time. "Some sort of funny business if you ask me," she said at last.

"I have a good mind to send her to the convent."

"What a feather in the Strathallan cap that would be!"

"Yes, I suppose it would," admitted Meredith.

"Near Aunt Ruby's place is a school where Cassie goes," said Tansy. "They have play lunch instead of eleven o'clock and the boys are in a different place and wear knickerbockers. I could go there if I was with Aunt Ruby."

"I see Ruby comes in for due mention," said Aunt Jessie.

"Yes, Ruby set herself about to please."

"Trying to get at him through her, is she?"

"Oh, her salad days are over, I should think," said Meredith. "Tansy, put a stick under the kettle and make Aunt Jessie a good, strong cup of tea. She makes a good cup of tea for a child of her age."

Meredith put the report away, but next morning Tansy asked for it.

"Why do you want it?"

"To show Cuthie."

"Oh, if you must," sighed Meredith, "but please, please don't show it to the Hogans or anyone you meet on the way."

Cuthie's reaction was unexpected. She was sitting at the table eating her breakfast when Tansy arrived, but having read the report she had to stand up and hold her sides. "You'll get away with murder, you will," she cried delightedly.

Tansy went home offended. She had no wish to murder anyone. It was well known that she was tender-hearted. She could not bear to see an ant squashed and during the mice plague had risen early each morning to rescue them. Meredith caught the mice in a big tub of water into which they slipped from the greased bottles around it. Those still swimming Tansy lifted out, took into the sun and dried, giving them warm milk and crumbs of cheese to revive them.

"Cuthie laughed at me," she told Meredith.

"Did she? That might teach you to show only the best side of yourself to people."

For the life of her Tansy couldn't see anything wrong with

the report. It didn't diminish her interest in school life; but it removed the heartening interest of her elders, who now preferred to talk of anything else instead.

Dolores was top of the class. The next few afternoons when Tansy came in, Meredith said, "Oh dear! I am behind with my sewing. Mrs Rowlands was over again. I haven't time to spare for that sort of thing."

"What sort of thing, Mother?"

"A lot of foolish chatter about children. Mrs Rowlands appears to have little in her own life to satisfy her. She derives her satisfaction from her children."

In time, however, Meredith consoled herself with the viewpoint that Tansy was in the same class as Dolores anyway; and as she was two years younger, she was therefore two years ahead.

Besides, Tansy had other attributes, according to Meredith. She saw things.

The passion vines Meredith had planted when she first came to the house had grown up, enclosing the verandahs, trained either side of the back and front steps to leave a natural doorway. Meredith liked this look, though Grand-dad was always warning her that vines rotted wood and could harbour snakes.

The water-bag hung under the vines in a corner of the front verandah. One lunchtime, before returning to school, Tansy went towards the bag for a drink of water but saw beside it, stretched up through the vines, a red-bellied snake, its head towards the top of the bag. Instead of telling Meredith she ran off to school and spent the afternoon in fear her mother would be bitten. She saw it all, Meredith going towards the bag, singing as she went, her hand stretching for the cup, the snake's head striking out.

"Pay attention, Tansy, please. Or is there something the matter?"

"There may be something up at home, Miss Peacebody."

"Well, would you like to run home and see?"

"No, Mother wants me to stop in the afternoons as you said."

"Don't look as if you're seeing ghosts then, child."

When school was let out Tansy did not go home but loitered about the town. However, with darkness there was nothing else for it. When she arrived everything appeared to be in order. The snake, as far as she could see, was gone. Marny was in her high chair beating impatiently with her spoon, Meredith sang "In the shade of the old apple tree" as she skimmed the fat from the top of the beef tea.

"Where were you after four?" she demanded of Tansy.

"Nowhere. Mother, was there a snake here?"

"There was. Ugly brute and I hope the other one isn't around. I had to get Mr Stone to bring his gun and shoot it. That's when it's hard not having a man about. It's on the ant-heap outside Roachtown now."

"Still wriggling?"

"No, not now. The sun's down."

"It must have made a lot of pieces, a big snake like that."

"It blew into five. Seven feet two inches from its wicked head to the tip of its tail." Then she looked at Tansy. "Did you see that snake before you went to school? Why ever didn't you tell me? I could have been bitten. Or Marny. To think of Marny being bitten —"

Tansy shuddered with Meredith. "No, I didn't see it," she said; "I just felt a snake was there."

"Where?"

"In the corner of the vines, by the water-bag."

"You felt that, you say?"

"Yes; and I felt it was a very big one. I sort of saw it, too. Miss Peacebody said, 'Don't look as if you're seeing ghosts, child.' "

"Good gracious!" exclaimed Meredith. "You're uncanny."

Tansy accepted Meredith's version of the episode and a few

weeks later, when she saw something else in school, she believed that too.

One afternoon a storm came up. The sky was green, chain lightning flashed, thunder rolled, the wind blew, it hailed. She had heard about bad storms from Grandfather. In one he had been in the dunny which blew over. In another his horse had been struck beneath him. She knew roofs blew away; whole houses went, helpless as thistledown in a breeze before the wrath of the wind; people died.

Suddenly she saw their house blow away, Meredith, Marny, machine, cotton reels and all with it. They would never be seen again. She was alone in the world.

By four o'clock the sun was shining, the afternoon fresh and fair as if nothing had ever been. But Tansy couldn't go home. She had no home, no mother singing "The saucy little bird in Nellie's hat" over the machine, no Marny playing with cotton reels.

She did not think of Cuthie or Aunt Jessie. By a trick of her mind they were as blown away from memory in the same way as Meredith and Marny.

She went at last to Knightbridges', a family with whom Grandfather had been friendly at one time. They lived in a large house past the old convent. As a very small child Tansy had gone there several times with Grandfather, but otherwise she barely knew them.

Mrs Knightbridge was a tall, quiet woman kept busy by eleven children of her own. She was surprised to see Tansy and took a while to identify her.

"Have you come for the afternoon?" she asked.

"No. To stay!"

"To stay! For how long?"

"For good."

"But why?" A humorous half-smile played about Mrs Knightbridge's thin mouth. Her life was spent with her own children and she was never too busy or too tired to enter into their make-believe in a calm and quiet way.

But the smile faded as Tansy said, "Mother and Marny are dead."

"Good gracious, child! What happened?"

"Our house blew away in the storm."

Mrs Knightbridge looked at her. "How did you escape, then?"

"I was at school."

Mrs Knightbridge raised her voice. "Francey, Francey," she called.

"Coming, Mum."

"Run down and see what has happened to Mrs Strathallan and the baby."

Francey ran off, and a girl of Tansy's own age called Josie was brought along to play with her.

Tansy liked Josie, and they played happily, but not for long. Francey was soon back to report that Mrs Strathallan and the baby were alive and well. Tansy was to go home at once.

Relieved and happy, Tansy went home. Meredith said nothing. She was too flabbergasted.

12 Caroline Cuthbertson's life had not been as the Lord intended. Or rather, the Lord had pointed in one direction and she had gone in another.

Not that she had been unhappy; oh dear no! What troubled her, as she sat on her front verandah one spring evening, was that suddenly she saw plainly that all her life she had set herself above the Lord. She had not waited to see what He was going to do with her but had chosen for herself. This had led her on varied paths till at last she had built herself a little house in which to settle down and await cheerfully a Christian end.

But she had anticipated the Lord in this matter, too. To wait cheerfully one has to feel like dying. She did not. The blood ran freely in her veins. Her heart and mind were as restless as ever. But what did an old woman do with herself?

These thoughts led her mind to another matter as she watched her little garden fade with the light, white moths fluttering in the dusk. All her life she had professed to believe in the church. What came to her now was that she had only believed in a type of church. The Lord had set down Low Church in the town of Goombudgerie and because she had always believed in High Church she had refused to have any part in it. There she went again!

This revelation was too much to keep to herself. Leaving the doors and windows wide open so that any wandering burglar could help himself to Queen Victoria or the teak box that had been her own dear mother's tea chest, the lamp burning low on the sitting-room table at the mercy of any fickle breeze which might blow up, she set out to find Meredith immediately.

Meredith was sitting on her front steps and heard Tansy, who was catching moths under a nearby lamp post, greet Cuthie. She saw them both come hurrying and stood up, alarmed. Something must be the matter.

"What is it, Cuthie?"

"Meredith," called Cuthie, breathless, "I see what it is I have to do. This is my town, that is my church, and he is my Rector. I must accept it."

"Accept what?"

"Church. I must go to church. I must be punished for wilfulness. It's what the Lord means. I couldn't see it before."

"Is that all that brought you hurrying over?" asked Meredith.

"All!" exclaimed Cuthie. "It's the sum total of my thoughts for the last six months and it means a lot to me."

"Come and sit down. You've knocked yourself up."

"I am blown out," admitted Cathie, "but my spirit is light. I'll see it through to the bitter end."

Tansy's heart sank. She knew that if Cuthie were seeing anything through to the bitter end, she would have to see it through, too.

"Which service, Cuthie?" she asked.

"The lot," replied Cuthie promptly. "Early morning, matins and evening. When I do a thing, I do it. I will take my meals here, Meredith. Save my legs a bit."

Meredith's heart sank. Sunday was her free day. She spent most of it reading. Now she would be tied to the hot stove instead.

One of the first outcomes of the Lord's intentions in regard to Cuthie was that Meredith found herself with a new dining room.

It was Cuthie's opinion that it did Meredith good to have to cook Sunday dinner. It gave her a chance to use the many nice things which she rarely brought out. On the other hand Meredith had much to say about the tablecloth and serviettes in the wash, and silver having to be cleaned.

Despite Meredith's complaints Tansy was pleased to have a Sunday hot meal as Dolores and everyone else had. Meredith, left to herself, was not interested in food. She had seen too much of it as a child at Land's End, she said. What she liked was bread and butter; Tansy felt she had seen too much of that. All the same, Meredith, when put to it, cooked well. Cooking was in the family, Cuthie said. No Cuthbertston or Trenworth turfed out unappetising meals. So the dinners pleased Cuthie.

Cuthie arrived early each Sunday morning to make sure Tansy was ready. She wore her best for church, black satin waist, black satin skirt loose-pleated and drawn into a band over buckram, black jet beads with silver cross attached, cameo and locket, black satin hat lined with pale pink beneath the brim. She carried the wooden-handled cloth bag which contained her Bible, prayer book and hymnal, Pap's umbrella and her handbag with her best Irish linen handkerchief peeping from the outside pocket. On her hands were black mittens crocheted by herself. The shops no longer sold them and she did not like her fingers restricted by gloves. With the fairness of her complexion, etched only lightly by wrinkles, offset by the black satin, she made a fine, upstanding figure, a finer, more upstanding figure than any other great-grandmother in that town. Cuthie knew it and was proud of it. So was Tansy. Cuthie gave her the feeling that life was permanent and stable.

She sat down for a rest while Tansy had tea and bread and butter. Cuthie, despite Meredith's protests, would eat nothing. This had something to do with High Church and Meredith thought it nonsense. Cuthie, with nothing in her stomach, would faint right away in church one of these mornings. During service Tansy watched anxiously to see if this was going to happen. Cuthie never showed signs of doing any such thing. She made noises in her throat, looked at Tansy and shook her head. Very dull, that service. Very Low — No music, no vestments, and flowers poor most of the year.

On the way home she voiced her complaints. She started with the Rector, whom she blamed for the service, and ended with Mrs Rowlands, whom she held responsible for the flowers.

Home to breakfast: Cuthie, hungry by this time, needing porridge, two eggs to her bacon and toast and marmalade.

"A hotel couldn't provide more," said Meredith.

They were back at church at ten-thirty, matins this time. They had their own seat, Cuthie having claimed the third row back on the left-hand side, as close as she could get after the churchwardens and a family from the country who sat in the second seat left as if by natural right. There were five in the family so they took the whole seat, blocking Cuthie's view of the lectern. That Rector had to be seen to be followed. It was fortunate that she knew the lessons and was able to follow by whispering them with him. Tansy was embarrassed but hoped that Cuthie's sibilant whisperings would be taken by the members of the congregation as the buzzings of a blowfly. She was too fond of Cuthie to have her held up to ridicule the way Holy Joe was. Say she began to be called "Holy Cuthie"? It would be unbearable.

The Rector's sermons grew worse and worse and longer and

longer. Sunday school was after matins and Cuthie had Tansy enrolled immediately. She attended with her for the first few Sundays and in this manner discovered that Tansy's Biblical knowledge was very poor.

"I don't know what your mother's been thinking about," she said as they went home. "I will have to attend to it myself."

So Tansy's pleasure in Sunday dinner was diminished by the knowledge that the long afternoon lay ahead and she had to share it with Cuthie and the Bible. They started at the beginning. "In the beginning God created the heaven and the earth. And the earth was without form, and void; and darkness was upon the face of the deep. And the Spirit of God moved upon the face of the waters."

Cuthie's voice droned on through the afternoon quiet of the house. The clock ticked, a blowfly buzzed. Tansy passed into a state between waking and sleeping where she lived a pleasant life of her own, being careful to keep her eyes wide open and fixed on Cuthie at the same time.

Meredith and Marny retired to the back verandah during these sessions. Meredith, with Marny dozing in the crook of her arm, lay on the stretcher and read the afternoon away.

In time Tansy grew to be what Cuthie called the flower of the Sunday school. She outstripped Dolores, whose mother, head of the Mothers' Union as she was, couldn't understand it. If Cuthie's schoolroom experience had been greater, Tansy might have been the flower of the school as well.

One June day Marny became four, a sound and solid four with views of her own, who could no longer be thought of as a baby.

"It seems but yesterday she was born," said Meredith. "How time goes! And we don't grow younger!"

No, they were all older. Tansy at nine had olden days herself now and could marvel with Meredith at the swift passage of the years.

Marny was perfect. "She has no blemish," Meredith said.

Marny was fresh and sweet. She had soft, fine hair the colour of Assam silk cut in a bob. Tansy loved it where the fringe made a straight line against the white of her forehead, the whiteness of the nape of her neck below her hair. Her eyes were bluer than those of any little girl they knew, her cheeks rounded and a faint, clear pink. Her mouth was beautiful, the top lip curved back, the bottom lip with a firm pout in the middle. Her teeth were square and white, well-spaced.

Tansy inspected these attributes of Marny's unsparingly, going over them one by one. She was devoted to the backs of her knees, the chicken bones in her wrists and the warm hollows in her collar bones. And she had a little pointed chin which stuck out and invited biting. If Tansy was specially nice to Marny she would say, "You can bite my chin. But not off."

Tansy felt she had done very well in the way of a little sister. This wasn't surprising. They had the best of everything apart from money. Money didn't matter. It was amazing how little one could get along on, supplemented by tins of eggs, vegetables, fruit and an occasional side of lamb from Land's End.

Cuthie surveyed her god-daughter one day and went to Meredith "I promised at her baptism to see she grew in the church. It's time she started and you with her. You need more outdoor activity."

"I don't," replied Meredith; "besides, with the sewing and the children and so much cooking I've no time to spare. As to Marny, she's a good little girl who can outsit most things, but I doubt if even she could stand one of the Rector's sermons. And you know what she's like about organs."

When they were out at Land's End, Grand-dad and Marny still retired to the horse trough during the Sunday afternoon hymn session. From that distance she liked the organ reasonably well.

"That's right," said Cuthie gloomily. "The church organ wouldn't do her, Miss Heany playing with all stops out to drown the choir, which is in itself a good thing but murders the music. It's a pity you can't go, Meredith. You would meet

136

more people. There might be someone who would take an interest in you.''

"What do you mean?" asked Meredith.

"You're a young woman still and a little passing interest never hurts anyone. Besides it could lead to something in the long run.''

"I don't know if you mean what I think you mean," said Meredith distantly, "but I happen to be a married woman and well aware of my duty.''

"Oh, duty falls before a lively interest.''

"Not with me, Cuthie. I'm surprised at you mentioning such a thing. Please don't do so again.''

"Very well; but I still think it would do you good.''

"I'm contented as I am. And if I did want something further in my life I doubt if I'd go to church to find it.''

Young girls met strange men in places other than churches, Meredith well knew. Whether this was the Lord's inattention or not didn't bother her. She rather thought the trouble lay with young girls themselves. They could be very careless of their destiny. But she excused them on the basis that it was better to love carelessly than not at all. And having loved, have done with it. Meet someone to take an interest in her, indeed!

Shortly after Tansy's birthday, the amaryllis wilted on its stem, the two pairs of openwork socks Aunt Ruby had sent still in their tissue, news came that the Rector was to be moved.

He had worked hard for the new church to be built, but he was not to have a fine brick edifice among the silky oaks. The money for the new church had come in slowly and it was only half-built.

Cuthie was upset. It turned out that she had grown fond of the Rector, poor sermons and all. She remained upset until suddenly, like Tansy, she saw something. She saw it in the middle of a weekday morning and came over as she was, in her houseclothes, a full dark skirt and mauve crepe blouse with her cameo brooch on the neckband to tell Meredith.

"Meredith," she said, "remember when Tansy and I were

away and the Archbishop laid the foundation stone? Well, the Archbishop was High. He saw the rector's Lowness and was displeased with it. The Rector is as good a man as God ever made, but one can't deny his Lowness. It won't do for the new church. The Archbishop will send a High man in his stead. Mark you, Meredith, that's how it will be! I feel it and I know it. It's my reward for putting up with the other."

"I thought rewards were in heaven," murmured Meredith.

Cuthie ignored this. "Church will be more interesting and the crowd will grow. Now, I don't want strangers in my seat. You will have to come, Meredith, to fill it up."

"But Cuthie —"

"Marny is quite old enough. And it won't be like one of *his* sermons. There's nothing like a good, sharp sermon to instruct a child properly."

"We'll see later," said Meredith.

"No; you'll have to come now."

"Oh, very well. If you're so set on it I'll do it to please you."

"Not to please me, Meredith; to please yourself," said Cuthie firmly. "Now where is Marny? I'm going to cure this organ business. Marny, Marny, come with Cuthie. She's taking you to hear the music."

Every day after that Cuthie took Marny to her place and played her little organ to her. All stops in, some stops out, all stops out, till Marny came to like it best with all stops out, Cuthie pedalling furiously.

She stood beside Cuthie, her elbow on Cuthie's knee, and learnt to sing "Nearer My God to Thee". Tansy listened anxiously, trying to detect something wrong with her singing. But she couldn't. She could hardly wait for the day when Miss Harriet would hear Marny's voice.

"You sang it beautifully, Marny," Miss Harriet would say.

Cuthie had her head high that first Sunday morning when she made her way down the aisle with all the Strathallan family behind her. Marny and Tansy were in new white voiles, six inches of lace on the bottom, rows of tucks and insertion, Marny's over pink Jap silk, Tansy's over blue. Wide pink and blue sashes tied in large bows at the back, fringed ends hanging to the lace hems. Straw hats with pink or blue ruche under the brims, bunches of pink or blue ribbons and daisies on the crowns. Pink or blue socks and black patent Mary Pickford shoes, named after the famous film star. Meredith's black-and-white checked costume had been shortened, skirts had gone up so. She wore her straw sailor with the spotted veil close to her face with the air of one wearing a new hat. It was not Meredith's hat which was outmoded but every other hat in church.

Mrs Rowlands also took pride in this family appearance and smiled at them from the choir. In the churchyard afterwards she came up to Meredith and said, "Marvels will never cease."

"What did she mean by that?" queried Meredith. "I belong to the church as much as she does. More so. I was born here."

"What did you think of the service, Meredith?" asked Cuthie.

"Very poor," replied Meredith promptly. "All you said and more so. How Marny sat still all that time, I don't know. And after all, though it was the church it is now the parish hall. It didn't feel like a church to me."

"Where two or three are gathered together," said Cuthie sternly.

Soon the Sunday school had a kindergarten, known as River Jordan, as its chief feature was a sand tray with the River Jordan flowing through the middle. Sometimes it turned into the road to Jerusalem, with two camels and a palm tree upon it; but as playing with water was more popular, it was mostly the River Jordan.

Marny was the first pupil enrolled and Tansy was given the pleasure of seeing her safely home. As there was no little girl in town as lovely as Marny it was a great joy to escort her home with everyone looking. But Dolores insisted on coming with them. Having no little sister of her own she set about stealing the affections of Tansy's. And Marny lapped the whole thing up and bestowed her love upon Dolores. It was Dolores' hand to which she clung when they walked across the bridge. Dolores came right into the house with them, delivering her to Meredith at the hot stove in the kitchen. "Here she is, Mrs Strathallan, safe and sound."

"Thank you, Dolores, but where is Tansy?"

"Marny won't hold her hand; she likes to hold mine."

"It was good of you, Dolores."

"It was no bother, Mrs Strathallan. I love doing it. She's so sweet."

"They don't come sweeter," admitted Meredith.

For the remainder of his stay everyone was very fond of the Rector. They remembered he had been christening and marrying and burying members of their families for years. They remembered that, however inconvenient to himself, he had never failed to answer a call. In summer heat and winter wind he had made long journeys across the plains to reach the sick. It was the Rector who was always first across the flooded river. He had not neglected to call on every one of his parishoners however far away their homes were. Who was it who was always there when anyone was in trouble? The Rector. No one blamed him any more about Hubert. Hubert was a pity for the Rector, that was all.

Like Cuthie, Tansy had become fond of the Rector and was sorry to see him go. But she was relieved about Hubert. The danger of marrying him was over now. The Rector could no longer refer to her as "my little daughter-to-be!"

The new church was finished in time to receive the new Rector. He was High, undoubtedly. So High that Cuthie kept her distance and devoted her energies to beautifying the new church. She wrote to people who had left the district, pointing out that as they had seen the beginning of the church here, they might like to give something to make the new church beautiful.

Cuthie was well supplied with catalogues from church supply stores, from which she advised donors what to give. While looking through one of these catalogues, she came upon the reproduction of a stained-glass window depicting two little angels with tangled curls and rosy cheeks. "Look, Meredith, look," said Cuthie; "aren't they the image of Eddie and Johnnie as they were the night they went?"

"I don't know, Cuthie. I wasn't born so I didn't see them."

"It's them all right, so close you can't tell the difference anyway. It's a good window if you can go by the cost, which is the highest in the book. I'll write and put it to Catherine. It would be better if she bought this window, instead of always hoping that the bones will be found so she can have a tombstone for them. Now her heart will be at rest at last."

Cuthie wrote to Granny Trenworth; but the river was up, or so she thought, Granny's reply taking some time. But finally Cuthie appeared waving a letter. "She's had a piece of both of us, Meredith," cried Cuthie cheerfully.

"Oh, has she?" queried Meredith. "Now, what could I have done?"

"You'll see. Holds things in, does Catherine, but comes out with them sometime, however long after."

In her letter Granny said that wool was down, not up as some seemed to suppose. Shearers now wanted a shower, no less, to their quarters, which had to be put there as they didn't grow. The price of bag sugar and flour had risen out of all bounds. She had spent a lot of money on Tansy that time she had her, all for nothing, the child went around as big a disgrace as ever with yards of bare legs showing. As to the other matter it had better rest till times were better. She was still hopeful for the tombstone, which she would prefer; it was her business, no one else's. Besides, wouldn't it be disquieting for Cuthie, seeing the angels there, recognising them and remembering? She had been minding them that night, hadn't she?

She ended, "I hear the new Rector isn't standing any nonsense. If he's not standing any nonsense, no one else need. Your devoted daughter, Catherine Trenworth."

"Well! Well!" said Meredith.

"Well! Well! Indeed!" said Cuthie; "but she needn't think the matter ends there. They cannot be gainsaid, those angels."

In time the two little angels appeared on the window by the Cuthbertson seat, third back on the left-hand side in the new church. Eddie and Johnnie in their nightshirts, curls tangled from their tubbing, cheeks rosy from the fire as they were that dreadful night they had vanished from the barn roof. Now they had haloes above their curls, they held golden harps, and their bare toes rested on a scroll: "Suffer the little children to come unto Me, and forbid them not, for of such is the kingdom of heaven."

Tansy and Marny loved them, their little lost uncles.

At third communion, which had taken the place of matins, the sun shone through the window, lovely dapplings of blue and purple and orange falling on the seat, Marny earnestly trying to pick them up.

"You can't pick them up, silly."

"Why?"

"They're not there."

"Does Dolores say?"

"No, I say."

"Be quiet, children. It's you, Tansy. Marny wouldn't start off by herself."

"*Hist*," from Cuthie.

But on the whole Mrs Cuthbertson was happy in her grand-daughter and great-granddaughters and the wonderful changes that had come about.

She was now alive again. The good times came again if one lived long enough. It was foolish of people to die and miss so much. "Hallelujah! Hallelujah!" sang Cuthie, loud in praise and happiness.

In came the choir behind: "Hallelujah! Hallelujah!"

13 There were no facts of life at Tansy's place. None whatsoever. No cabbages or birds and bees.

But of course they filtered through.

Dolores was first with the news. She called to Tansy from her front gate one Saturday morning. "Look here, Tansy, if you're not doing anything and if your mother doesn't want you, I'll let you come to the dentist with me.

"I don't mind," Tansy said. Dolores always liked someone to go with her, while when Tansy went anywhere she liked to go by herself.

When they reached Dolores on the bridge, she said, "I could tell you something if I liked, but I don't know if I will or not."

"Oh yes, Dolores, please tell?"

"Well, I'll see. I'll have to think about it. I am two years older than you are."

"But I'm in the same class."

"This is different," said Dolores; "what I mean is at my age I'm still too young to know, so as you're younger than me —"

"Who told you?"

They were passing the bakehouse and Aunt Jessie came down the steps. "I've got a nice fresh cinnamon," she said amiably. "Going along the street? I am too." Up went Aunt Jessie's parasol.

"Dolores has something to tell," said Tansy.

"Oh, no, I haven't," said Dolores hastily.

Ah! Tansy realised. It was something of S-H-I-T on walls sort.

"I turn down here," Aunt Jessie said.

"So do we," said Dolores. "I'm going to the dentist's."

"Ah, dentists. Save what you've got. If I'd been able to get near a dentist at your age I'd still have my own teeth."

Aunt Jessie bade them farewell outside the dentist's. Off she went in her violet print, black shoes and stockings, parasol upraised, square basket with the cinnamon in it over her arm. Now Dolores could tell.

However, when they were alone in the waiting room, instead of telling Dolores said, "Isn't it dreadful?"

"What?"

"What they do."

"What who does?"

"Your mother and father. Oh my goodness! Now that is a mystery. When does your mother see your father?"

"When she goes up north."

"When's that?"

"She can't go now. Grandfather's dead and there's Marny. Besides, she doesn't want to. She's done with that sort of thing."

"I should think so. A long way to go for it. I suppose that explains things in a way, but it's still rather strange. However, we'll let your father go. But when it comes to my father it doesn't seem possible."

"What?"

"What he does."

"When?"

"Five times. Awful, isn't it? I can hardly bear it. As to why Mother allowed it I don't know. But she did. Here am I to tell the tale. *And* James and John and Beatrice and Dalzell."

The dentist appeared in the doorway of the surgery. "Ha! I've caught you again, young lady."

"Oh, Mr Brocklehurst, you're not going to hurt, are you?"

"Only a little. Worth it, you know, for all those ivory castles in your head."

"Yes, Mr Brocklehurst, it's only when it's happening I don't like it." Dolores was ushered in, all smiles and dimples.

Tansy waited all that long time. When Dolores came out she asked, "What was it you were going to tell?"

"But I told you, stupid."

"Oh, that!"

"Yes that! Bad enough, isn't it! Come on home and don't say a word. If you breathe one word, I'll murder you." So they went down the steps and through the gate and onto the street.

144

"But where does it come out?" asked Dolores imploringly. "It couldn't come out there. It just could not."

Dolores' news was baffling; but in time, combined with other things, it gave a lead.

When Tansy did not know the meaning of a word Meredith always said, "Go to the dictionary." So Tansy took *pregnancy* to the dictionary, and a very jolly book the dictionary proved to be, straightforward if a little less detailed than she could have wished. Meredith was pleased with this real interest Tansy was taking in her studies.

"Why on earth has Tansy always got her head in the dictionary?" Cuthie demanded. From the way Cuthie said it, Tansy felt Cuthie had her own ideas about dictionaries.

"She's attending to her spelling," said Meredith.

In a very short time Tansy was able to tell Dolores all about babies. "They grow in the womb," she said. "They do come out there and they happen after *intimacy* takes place." She had read about intimacy in the papers as well as the dictionary. In the cities a dark lane was mostly chosen, though it was hardly the place she would have chosen herself. In the reporting of several local court cases, the bench in the park Dolores had tut-tutted at that distant day came in for mention. A much more suitable place, she considered.

"Tansy! Fancy coming out with it like that!"

"Why not? It's true, isn't it?"

"But to say it! Don't you think it's horrible?"

"No. One must get used to the idea."

"But will you be able to face it when the day comes?"

"Why, certainly." A vision of the Hogan boy rose in Tansy's head and she had to dispel it quickly not to grow squeamish in front of Dolores. She certainly did not want *intimacy* with him.

"Tansy, you're awful, just awful! I know I'll shudder and shudder."

Being two years older, Dolores had had the benefit of every

day and was therefore top in class, but Tansy felt she had out-grown her.

She had.

That night she was drifting off to sleep when there was a step on the verandah. From her bed she recognised Mrs Rowlands' tall form outlined against the darkness and immediately had an idea of what had happened. Dolores had tattled again. She stayed where she was with her eyes closed.

Meredith suffered shock when disturbed at night, her mind spinning with the names of people who might be dead. "Tell me quickly," she greeted Mrs Rowlands, "who is it?"

"It's Dolores," said Mrs Rowlands.

"Oh, whatever happened, the poor child?"

"She is so upset I can hardly make head nor tail of her story. She —"

"She's not dead? That is a relief."

"Of course she's not dead! One thing I can make out is that Tansy told her the facts of life."

"The what?" asked Meredith.

"The facts of life. How one comes to be born."

"I've never heard it called that before," said Meredith. "Dear me! Are you sure it was Tansy?"

"You will have to find that out from her. In the meantime much harm has been done to Dolores. I'm not upbraiding you about it, Mrs Strathallan, but I feel you should know. These things are better squashed at the source."

"Indeed yes, but I feel you are mistaken in thinking it was Tansy."

The conversation went round in a circle for some time. Mrs Rowlands went at last, not entirely satisfied if one could judge by her coughs. Meredith held the lamp above Tansy and had a good look at her, but Tansy was sound asleep.

Meredith was not entirely satisfied either. Next morning she said, "Tansy, if that little cat, Dolores, ever told you some-thing that wasn't very nice, you wouldn't tell Marny, would you?"

"Oh, no, Mother. I never tell Marny anything that isn't nice.

"That's right," said Meredith, soothed. "Now run off to school. Is Mr McCarthy pleased with your spelling?"

"Yes; he's pleased with everything."

"Oh, darling, comb your hair before putting your hat on. Comb it through with water. A wild-rose appearance can be very pretty, but mostly it's just untidy." Meredith was peering at her intently, as if Tansy had a new face and she was seeing it for the first time. When Tansy's hazel eyes met her green ones she smiled uncertainly. Tansy had the uncomfortable feeling that her mother saw something different in her. She combed her hair swiftly, jammed on her hat and raced out of the hosue and through the gate.

On the other side of the road Dolores was waiting. She did not look at all upset.

"Hurry up, Tansy. I must be there by first bell. I'm always there by then."

"I'm going the other way. Goodbye!"

"Rude pig!" Dolores shouted after her. "You're everything Mother says you are."

Mother did, did she? Well, they weren't going to hamstring Tansy Strathallan. She'd talk about babies all she liked.

And who had started it all? Dolores! That day at the dentist's.

14 At the end of each school year the teacher sent Meredith a note to say that as Tansy was so young, it would be better if she stayed back a class the following year. But Meredith replied saying she thought it better for her to go up with the others; she had been with them all the way through and might miss them.

It wasn't as if she did badly in class, Meredith pointed out to Tansy. She had Tansy's word for that. It was just exams she couldn't seem to manage. Meredith doubted if she could have managed an exam herself. "Besides," Meredith said to Tansy, "once you're through fifth you'll be done with it all."

However, at the beginning of the year Tansy started in fifth class, a high school was attached to Goombudgerie school.

"Good Lord!" said Meredith, when the significance of this had sunk in. "It looks as if you have to go through that on top of all the other. It never stops."

Some of the women for whom Meredith sewed had children at the high school. They told her how expensive the books were and how many were needed. Then there was the uniform. As Mrs Strathallan sewed so beautifully, would she mind helping with a tunic? Make it look like a bought one, so no one would know? Of course Meredith didn't mind. She charged very little for these as the poor things were up for so much expense already and in an uncertain state as to what would happen to their girls afterwards. Would they go into the Shire or Town Council, one of the two attorneys' offices, or be taken away by the government to be made school teachers? A girl's destiny of staying home peacefully then getting married appeared to have been ruined by the high school.

Meredith didn't like the uniform either. It was hot and heavy. "If there's one colour you can't wear, Tansy, it's maroon," she mourned. "Why ever have they chosen it? You'll look like a boiled beetroot in summer."

What with Meredith making tunics cheaply, Marny and Tansy going through their sandals at the same time, the sanitary rate going up, and Mr Chaseling either charging more for goods or their eating more, it was a poor year.

"And all those books to come on top of it," said Meredith. "I really don't know which way to turn."

There was an exam to be passed before entering high school, but Meredith did not take it into account. The exam was in November. However, owing to much premature worry about books and uniforms, Meredith came to the end of her tether in October instead of November that year.

Just when she was, on her own admission, at her last gasp, Granny and Grand-dad Trenworth appeared in town.

"You look a fright, Meredith," said Granny. "I'd advise you to come home with us."

"What, today?"

"Why not?"

"I might have as I haven't any sewing in the house, but —"

"But what?"

"Well, the amaryllis comes out on Tansy's birthday —"

"Good gracious!" said Granny. "Is that all? Marny came out on her birthday and and left her violets to bloom by themselves. It's the nonsense you go on with, Meredith, which makes your life difficult."

Granny was in the mood to carry everything before her, and Meredith was in the mood to be carried away by anything. When Tansy and Marny came home at lunchtime they found themselves packed up and Meredith in the black-and-white checked costume ready to go to Land's End.

Out they went, leaving behind the amaryllis to bloom by itself and the school break-up where Marny was to have chanted "I'm a great big policeman", curtsied like a rose, worn her white dress in all the songs, said "Christopher Robin", and, as top of the Infants', undoubtedly received a prize.

They forgot all these things as they journeyed over the plain through the brassy light of the summer afternoon. The breeze whipped colour into their pallid town cheeks, the peace revived their jaded nerves. Only Tansy thought of the high school exam.

"I don't know how you put up with that jangle in Goombudgerie," Granny shouted at Meredith over the roar of Grand-dad's engine.

Grand-dad's Ford had been the first in the district. It would see him out, he said. However, it was beginning to cause his granddaughter shame. Other people bought new cars, why not Grand-dad? But, having led the way, his spirit of adventure had been satisfied. Besides, he was the sort of person who grew accustomed to what he had, and he didn't believe in discarding anything before it was worn out. Tansy was beginning to question these old-fashioned virtues.

They returned to Goombudgerie at the end of January, rested, eager to take up life in the town again.

Meredith admitted that she had grown out of country ways and became a town person. Tansy rather thought she had too. At Land's End you knew what was going to happen day by day; in Goombudgerie anything could happen. The fact that it rarely did didn't make any difference. A wider world interested mother and daughter more. It was all right for Marny, who went about the paddocks with Grand-dad and already had a working knowledge of the place.

Marny knew interesting things about footrot and worms; she knew how many sheep could be carried to the acre in a good season or a poor one. She knew Grand-dad's opinion of taking sheep to sales and markets in railway trucks instead of the pleasanter, slower method of droving. And Grand-dad had given her a windmill as a Christmas present. Of course Meredith and Tansy had had the same opportunities, but their minds weren't attuned in the same way. So they were caught up with Granny and the housework, which, instead of becoming less, as it should have been, became heavier, Meredith believed.

The mail car, now running two days a week between Derrick Plains and Goombudgerie, set them down at their own gate. They opened their own front door and life caught up with them immediately.

"Mice," said Meredith, sniffing. "I wonder how much has been chewed."

They threw open the doors and windows. As usual the house seemed small after Land's End, an insubstantial box of cypress pine, the varnished furniture sparse and shabby, the curtains hanging limply, desolate. A house was a shell without inhabitants.

"The part of 'Lalla Rookh' I was reading is gone," said Tansy. "I left the book open there, when we went."

"Never mind," said Meredith, "what you know is enough." "Lalla Rookh" had drifted from the graveyard to the house at Land's End, disturbing Granny. Meredith had explained so often that all growing girls took a turn for poetry and grew out of it that she was tired of it.

She went outside and knocked the rungs of the tank. "I think someone has made off with some of our water. And don't the fowls look seedy? Those Hogan children haven't fed them properly. How many fowls did we have, Tansy?"

"Nine, Mother."

"We have eleven now. Bring in some chips and we'll get the kettle on."

Lighting the fire in the stove, Meredith said, "This isn't drawing properly. I suspect the top of the flue is going. Of course it could be a swallow's nest again. I'll borrow Stone's ladder later and have a look. That's where a man in the house is helpful. They can do those things so easily."

"I'll go up the ladder, Mother."

"We won't worry about it now. Get a pencil and paper and we'll make out a list for Chaselings' — was that our gate?"

Tansy left the kitchen and passed through the dining room to the passageway where she had a clear view. "Yes, Mother. It's Mrs Rowlands."

"Oh bother!" exclaimed Meredith. "So soon."

With Mrs Rowlands were Dolores and Dalzell. Dolores had Marny's school prize.

"Oh, thank you, Dolores," said Meredith.

"It was no bother, Mrs Strathallan. I went up for it myself. Oh dear, it was funny! It was the Member himself, not his representative who gave out the prizes. He said to me, 'I'm not surprised you're top of the Infants.' So I explained about it; and the next thing Annie Ashgrove's name was called out, and I knew she was down with the mumps, so I had to go up and get hers. Then I had to go up and get all my own prizes."

"So the Member and Dolores were old friends by the time it was over," said Mrs Rowlands; "but that's not what I came about. A few days before we left for the seaside, in the middle of packing in fact, a gentleman came to my door and asked if I knew where you were."

"Oh!" said Meredith.

"I take it he was your husband," said Mrs Rowlands.

Meredith considered. She looked into the distance, then brought her eyes back to Mrs Rowlands' face. "If a man asked for me it would be my husband, Mrs Rowlands," she said.

"I knew so!" exclaimed Mrs Rowlands. "I told him nothing had been vouchsafed me; that you had vanished overnight, here one day, no smoke from the chimney the next."

"Did he leave a message?" asked Meredith.

"Yes, that he hadn't seen you up north lately."

"He knows very well," said Meredith, "that I will not take the children into that climate."

"I should think not," said Mrs Rowlands; "we bear them, we have the pain and trouble and it's for us to say what is best for them. It's a pity you missed him."

"A great pity," said Meredith.

"Can I lend you anything, Mrs Strathallan, as you've been away so long?"

"No thank you, Mrs Rowlands, but I'll have to get busy. Mice and cockroaches have taken over, I'm afraid."

The Rowlands went. "Well, that was a dash of cold water," said Meredith. "It was a blessing all round that we were at Land's End. But why must he go to Mrs Rowlands? However, he seems to have behaved nicely."

But Mrs Rowlands had not been as taken with George as all that. When Tansy was going to Chaselings' Dolores joined her.

"Wait on, Tansy; I'll come with you, if you like. I haven't seen you for ages. I say, your father is a queer customer, isn't he? Mother didn't know if he was your father or not. She thought he might be one of those people who spy out the land then burgle the place at night."

Tansy was indignant. She had heard much about George and nothing to his credit, but never that he stole things. She told Dolores so. "Besides, there's nothing in your house to steal," she said. "And another thing. I don't like the way your father sneezes. I could not put up with it!"

"You have never been the same, Tansy Strathallan, since you found out ALL THAT."

"No; it changes one," said Tansy.

When Tansy returned home, Cuthie was there. Tansy assumed that Cuthie had seen George too and come to tell them about it. However, Cuthie's contribution was different altogether.

"Tansy," said Meredith reproachfully, "Cuthie says you can't go to high school. You have not passed the exam."

"That's right," said Cuthie. "I'm not mentioning it to be disparaging but to save your mother making a tunic you won't be wearing. I saw the names of those who passed in the *Bi-weekly Star* and, when your name wasn't there, rang my friend to see why. He said you hadn't passed and that was flat, there was no mistake at all. And you can't get into the high school without an entrance."

"But I didn't sit for the exam," said Tansy.

"You have always taken exams far too lightly," said Meredith. "There must be something in them or they wouldn't have them. Now what are we going to do?"

"I'll leave school and help you," said Tansy airily. If she had sat for the exam she would have been quite prepared to be deflated by not passing; not having sat for it, she wasn't.

"You can't," said Cuthie. "That's another thing. The government says you have to stay there till you're fourteen. All she can do is go in the same class again and pass the exam next time."

"I hardly like that," said Meredith. "She's done it all before. There must be a way out."

"None that I can see," said Cuthie and took her departure.

"I'll never go for a holiday again," said Meredith. "Everything goes wrong the moment one is home."

"We could go to the seaside next time," said Tansy.

"We could not," said Meredith.

"Well, we could go to Sydney and stay with Aunt Ruby Buckland."

"Good gracious! What are you talking about?" demanded Meredith.

"Everyone goes somewhere," said Tansy fiercely.

"We've just been at Land's End for four months."

"Land's End is the same only worse."

"We should be thankful we have Land's End to fall back upon."

"I'm tired of being thankful about things."

"Who, you?" demanded Meredith. "You who can't do a very ordinary thing like passing a high school exam!"

"Oh, Mother," muttered Tansy.

"I am very pleased Dolores passed her exam," Meredith told Mrs Rowlands the next time she saw her. "I will do her tunic for you if it would be a help. I am told the tunics I made last year could pass for bought ones."

"They are rather better," said Mrs Rowlands. "That is very kind of you and I would accept your offer if Dolores were going to high school, but Dolores is going to the convent to take out a scholarship. You see, in our position we cannot allow a girl to continue on at the state school. We wish to send her to a church school in Brisbane to finish her education. As we have another one, a boy at that, to put through, the scholarship money will help considerably."

"Oh," said Meredith.

"Are you thinking of the same thing for Tansy? It would be nice after being friends for so long if they went off to Brisbane together."

"No," said Meredith regretfully. "I couldn't consider that for Tansy."

"But she could take out a scholarship," said Mrs Rowlands, "and when she has it go to the high school here, rejoining her own class in the middle of the year. The money will cover her books. It's what I'd do if I were you. Come and have a cup of tea and I'll explain more fully."

Meredith went, something in the nature of Grandfather's pension swimming before her eyes. Already the security of a steady income, however small, was creeping over her.

"I knew there was a way out," she said later. "Would you like to go to the convent, Tansy?"

"I think I'd like it," said Tansy. "Much better than going back into fifth at the state school."

The convent had fees. Sixpence a week. Rather steep on top of the fact that Tansy had to attend the Church of England three times on Sundays and now was so big she had to put threepence in the plate each time. There was also a uniform, but quite simple — navy blue frock with white piqué collar and cuffs.

"The sort of thing you look better in than maroon," said Meredith.

Sandals had to be black. Tansy had new brown ones, but Chaselings' would have something with which to do them over. There should be black socks but Meredith would have to think about that. She drew the line at hot, sticky socks in summer. They made the feet smell. She knew several people who, having worn thick, dark socks from childhood had never recovered from the complaint. There was also a large straw hat, natural in colour with a navy underlining; and a band, two and three-pence extra, which had on it an inscription in Latin. Meredith, having always been fond of Latin, liked that.

Cuthie was not consulted on these matters, but of course she heard. She came over to investigate. "What is this about Tansy going to the convent? It's all over town."

"She's going to take out a scholarship," explained Meredith.

"I know all about those scholarships," said Cuthie. "It's a way of making converts."

"That might be so," said Meredith, "but I'm too far involved to pull out."

Cuthie departed but Aunt Jessie arrived. "You are giving the Strathallans something to crow about," she said.

"They can crow their heads off," said Meredith. "I will not have that stand in Tansy's light."

Dolores and Tansy went together to their first day at the convent. Tansy began the day at the table behind the piano known as the scholarship class. She ended it in fifth, in the front seat, from where she would see the board nicely. She went home with a note to Meredith from Sister in which Sister said, in the pleasantest manner, that she did not think Tansy had sufficient grounding to face scholarship this year. It would be better to remain in fifth and do scholarship next year.

"Dear me!" said Meredith. "How much grounding does one need? You've had years of grounding." The years of Tansy's schooling rolled back and she felt that she had been on a battlefield where the skirmishes broke out in unexpected places and never came to a conclusion. She gave up. "Do you like the convent, Tansy?"

"Yes, Mother. And I have a new friend. We just looked at each other this morning and knew we liked each other better than anyone else. We've talked and talked all day." The lines between Meredith's mouth and between her brows settled deeper at that, her mouth compressed in disapproval. Tansy hurried on. "You know our Doctor John? She's his little girl, Janet. She's glad I've come, as she would have been the only Proddo in the class otherwise."

"The only what?"

"Protestant. That's what Janet and I are. You'll like Janet, Mother. She's much more suitable than Dolores, I think."

Meredith's mouth relaxed. "We're in this. We'll remain in it up to the hilt." They did.

15 "It's a pig," said Janet, "giving birth. I'm very interested in pigs."

"Why?" asked Tansy.

They were sitting on the verandah in the sunshine together.
From inside came the sound of the others droning away at their
catechism.

"They appeal to me," said Janet, and put the pig back between the pages of her history book.

"I suppose it's the same as humans," hazarded Tansy.

"Yes, but pigs have more."

Janet was interested in the facts of life only in a practical
way. "We get too much of them at home," she told Tansy,
"always cropping up in the middle of Daddy's meals or at
night. Do you know, I've never had a birthday party without
someone having a baby slap bang in the middle of it."

From nine-thirty till ten, from twelve till half-past, Janet
and Tansy had their lives together. Meredith, Cuthie and Aunt
Jessie all thought Janet a good friend for Tansy. And so she
was, Janet with the milk-white skin, the powdering of freckles
on her nose which crinkled when she smiled, the grey-blue eyes
under curling lashes, the wheaten curls on her neat little head
and her precise and practical way of handling everything. And
Doctor John thought Tansy a good friend for Janet. So everyone was happy, apart from Dolores, who, having known
Tansy for many years, having brought her to the convent and
not having made any new friends herself, felt Tansy should be
more faithful to days that were past. Tansy was, in her way,
but wondered why, when she liked Dolores and liked Janet,
they wouldn't like each other.

"Oh, her," Janet would say, crinkling up her nose.

"Doctors' daughters are too knowing, Mother says," was
Dolores' contribution. "I'm not to take any notice of anything
she might tell me."

Nevertheless Dolores attached herself to Tansy and Janet at
lunchtimes and would start a conversation on a subject about

which Janet knew nothing, and which showed her prior claim to Tansy.

"Remember the day your mother was making a sponge and we went to the park?"

Tansy, always willing to be drawn by olden days, couldn't help replying, "And I fell in the creek and took whooping-cough."

"And I pulled you out. Goodness me, Tansy, you wouldn't have been here now if I hadn't!"

At this Tansy smiled weakly. She was never sure if Dolores said this to impress Janet or really believed it. She knew she could have got out of the creek on her own account.

Lunchtimes were not a success and in the afternoons Dolores expected Tansy to walk home with her. Now and again Tansy gave her the slip and walked home Janet's way. Afterwards, while not wanting to, she found herself apologising to Dolores.

This unexpected seeming devotion on Dolores' part, and Tansy's own knowledge that she couldn't answer it fully, caused her a slight uneasiness, the only blemish on days that were otherwise perfect.

The convent was in what was considered the prettiest part of the town, if a town situated in the middle of a plain and laid out in square blocks, criss-crossed with streets can be considered to have a prettiest part. From the front one had a view of the creek where it dwindled and began to lose itself in the flat land westward. Nice open country, everyone said. It stood in large grounds, the boarding convent built of bricks facing one street, the school convent built of weatherboard raised high on tin-capped piles to resist the white ants facing another. The width of a wide playground lay between them. Trees, silky-oaks, maples and cedars made cool patches of shade. There were lawns and arbours, rock gardens and flower-beds.

The convent had music; pianos rippled, violins squee-awked, voices trilled all day long. It had painting; any girl was at liberty to join a class and unfold pink rose petals backed by glossy leaves on canvas; there was a library where anyone might choose a book provided she paid a penny and signed her name.

These wonders burst on Tansy along with the casual, undemanding affection of Janet's friendship. Her growing indifference to Dolores, a tendency to regard Dolores' attacks and outbursts as funny, worried her only as a sense of disloyalty. Her loyalty to Dolores and to the "olden days" remained when all else had fled.

Janet sat tenth in class and Tansy was bottom, which was much too far apart. It only gave them catechism together, seeing lunchtime was marred by Dolores. Janet took the matter in hand.

"We have a monthly test and where you come is how you sit. Say we tie for fifteenth?"

"How can we do that?" asked Tansy, who had learnt not to aspire to any particular position in class.

"If we learn together we'll know the same things."

So they learnt together when outside during prayers and catechism, sitting in Doctor John's car outside the hospital, on the surgery steps, or on the seat Uncle Joe Sprockett had made for Meredith under one of the cedar trees in the Strathallan backyard.

"It's wonderful how Tansy has taken to it all," said Meredith.

But they couldn't learn all the time as they had so much to talk about. There were matters of procedure.

"Did you feel silly when you stood for the Pope?" asked Janet.

"No, I didn't mind," Tansy said. She considered. "I don't think I felt anything at all. Should I have, do you think? Last year when I was confirmed Cuthie said I would feel in a state of grace. But I didn't. I don't think I've ever felt in a state of grace."

"What's that got to do with the Pope?" asked Janet. "Ask you one thing, Tansy, and you start on another.

"It has to do with it," returned Tansy; "Tessie Moody was in a state of grace when she stood for the Pope. There was a rapt expression on her face."

"She always has an odd expression of some sort," said Janet. "And that's not what I mean. I didn't mind standing for the Pope as it happens to be his school and though it's not for the King it's not against him. It doesn't make us heretics."

"Traitors, wouldn't it be?" asked Tansy.

"Oh, one of those things," said Janet. "Let's learn this whole chapter of history word for word. If we keep on learning at this rate, towards the end of the year we should come top together. Then we'd get a medal on First Friday. Of course we'll get a good conduct medal before that. About June, I should say. It's obvious that the good Catholics must get them first. But we'll get ours before the bad ones. Sister is very fair."

Sister was. She was a tall Irishwoman with a thin-lipped, humorous mouth and keen, dancing eyes. She spoke in a clear, well modulated voice without trace of accent. It was the most English and most beautiful voice in Goombudgerie. Tansy had not heard one like it before and fell under its spell. It was from Sister that she heard her first fragments of the great poets, Sister not being above bringing a small volume from her pocket and refreshing them with something she liked herself if her pupils appeared to be wilting under the onslaught of a too matter-of-fact lesson.

Sister took an interest in her two young Proddos. They knew she liked them. She never made them feel outside the pale as some of their classmates took delight in doing. Every Monday morning she asked them if they had been to their own church the day before.

Having Cuthie, Tansy was always able to say, "Yes, Sister." Janet mostly said, "No, Sister; my father thinks a growing girl should rise at her leisure on Sunday mornings, but I will go some time to please you."

"Not to please me, Janet dear."

"Very well; I'll go to please the Bleeding Heart." At which

Sister raised her thin, beautiful white hands but said nothing further.

On occasional Sundays after that, to Tansy's great pleasure, Janet came scurrying into the seat beside Cuthie and herself, blessing herself hastily, and was able to say, "Yes, Sister," the next morning.

Cuthie's notions didn't go as far as blessing oneself, and she was upset by this habit of Janet's. "I must say Doctor John is bringing up that girl in a fashion all his own. I don't think she knows which church is which. And why hasn't she been confirmed? It wouldn't surprise me if she wasn't baptized."

"She is baptized," Tansy explained. "But she's to make up her own mind about confirmation. So far she hasn't felt like it."

"Indeed!" exclaimed Cuthie. "What a way to bring up a child."

Tansy felt privately that Janet was well brought up. She enjoyed hearing about Mummy and Daddy and the friendly life all three lived together.

"I suppose it's because there's three of you, you have such a good time," she said to Janet.

"Well, there's three of you," replied Janet cheerfully.

There were three of them, but it wasn't the same. Or perhaps Tansy only thought it wasn't.

When the results of the first monthly test came out, Tansy was a few marks behind Janet.

"Oh, dear!" said Sister. "There's something I had forgotten. You read so nicely, Tansy, I meant to give you extra marks for it. I daresay I can give them to you now. That makes you equal place with Janet, fifteenth. You've slipped a little, Janet. Are you finding the work difficult?" Sister's eyes twinkled.

"No, Sister," said Janet; "I mean, yes, Sister. But I've got the hang of it now. Tansy and I are working very hard and I think next time we should come twelfth. We only have to beat Tessie Moody and Terry Callaghan to do that."

"Spare my conscience," murmured Sister, and departed.

Meredith was pleased with Tansy's progress in her first month at the convent. "Tansy has not only passed her exam," she told Aunt Jessie, "but she has come fifteenth along with Janet. A very good position."

Meredith, used to the twenty-four class of the state school, had formed the opinion that there were twenty-four in all classes. There were seventeen in the convent class.

The convent had already had its effect in other ways. Not for the first time in her career, Tansy became made over almost immediately. The convent, like Granny Trenworth, wanted her skirts lengthened. They were lengthened; her knees disappeared. The convent wanted her hair brushed and off her forehead. It was brushed night and morning and held neatly in place with a blue ribbon. The convent wanted her shoulders straightened. She straightened them and appeared to grow taller. The large brim of her straw hat shaded her face; her tan faded to an interesting paleness.

Meredith often had to look twice when Tansy came sedately through the gate, shutting it carefully behind her, to make sure it was Tansy. The convent liked growing girls to behave like young ladies. Meredith did too. So did Cuthie, Granny and Aunt Jessie. But they didn't have the influence of the convent. When the convent put the matter to her, Tansy was so entranced with the idea that she gave her full attention to it for several months. By the time something else took her interest most of the habits had stuck.

While Cuthie, Granny and Aunt Jessie approved of the beneficial results of convent training, they were not pleased with Meredith for going over to the Strathallans and putting Tansy in the convent.

But Meredith stuck to her guns. "The convent has something," she said, "and I know just what it is. Man does not live by bread alone."

"That's all very well," said Aunt Jessie, "but how does he get on without it?"

*　*　*

As it happened it was as well Tansy had left the State school. It was all right for smaller girls like Marny, but not the place for big girls. Scandal broke loose in the upper levels. Tansy's one time friend, Miriam, put the young high school teacher into trouble and was asked to leave. Shortly afterwards she was to be seen about town with her very own baby. It was a dear little creamy baby with tight black curls. Miriam smiled dreamily above it, shooting glances from her lovely eyes at passers-by.

This event, which was the centre of public interest in Goombudgerie for several months (only Miriam, her parents and the baby appearing unconcerned over it), did not pass unnoticed by Tansy and Janet. A girl only a year or two older than themselves had had a baby, a girl moreover who had once been Tansy's friend. Tansy was bewildered rather than shocked by Miriam's rapid assumption of adulthood.

The upshot of Miriam's behaviour was that Meredith could no longer see her way clear to allowing Tansy to attend the State high school. Anything could happen there. As Tansy couldn't see her way clear to obtaining a scholarship, she agreed with her mother's decision.

She did not join the scholarship class at the beginning of the next year but went instead to the convent high school. Janet went too. She and Tansy kept each other company in first year. The pupils in the higher grades were boarders, big girls from properties farther west who had started their schooling late. Some were religious and some impatient to be off to the social life which waited for them outside. They had no interest in Tansy and Janet and left them alone.

"There's been a lot of to-do about nothing," said Cuthie when she heard of this news. "What did Tansy go to the convent for, if not to take out a scholarship?"

"To become educated," said Meredith firmly. "In my experience it's the only place that can do it. Sister is a wonderful woman and Tansy is devoted to her."

163

"What about Marny? Isn't she to be educated? She's my goddaughter, remember."

"She's too young yet but will go in her turn. Besides, she's taken to the State school as Tansy never did. Perhaps it was Tansy going through first which gave her an inkling."

"What nonsense!" said Cuthie. "She's different, that's all."

The convent high school, being small, was not as formal as the State school. Girls who grew too big for fifth were passed on there and remained a short or long time according to how their parents' sixpences or boarding fees held out. This process was known as being "finished off", and whether one remained six months or six years one was still "finished" when one left. A much more sensible idea, Tansy and Meredith felt.

Tansy came to rest, as it were, at the convent. The strife was o'er, the battle won. Meredith, like Tansy, was content to be done with the competitive part of schooling. "The pitting of one child against the other", she called it. When Meredith was a child she had learnt by herself, apart from the time in the convent, of which she didn't remember much, those tight shoes superseding all else. Many of those things had stuck and stood her in good stead later.

She had learnt to sew by herself, taking apart the wedding gown of Mrs Jeremy Grant Whittaker, which had come from Paris, and putting it together again. Where would she have been now without her sewing? Tansy wasn't sure where her mother would have been without this asset; but she wished that when Meredith had chosen to set herself up in a town, she had chosen a larger, more interesting one, Sydney preferably. Goombudgerie was spreading out, it was said, but it seemed to Tansy that it only spread out in the same manner, more houses which looked alike, more shops, another bank. However, her restlessness was swallowed for the time being by the convent high school.

The high school had its being in the prep room, the rec room and on the verandahs of the boarding convent. Being one of three brick buildings in the town, the convent had its own prestige. Like Aunt Ruby the people of Goombudgerie admired bricks. The convent building had an enduring feeling to Tansy; she loved the deep cool rooms, the wide passages, the staircase with its shining balustrade of polished wood. The building had space and dimensions, light and shadow; her spirit knew freedom without walls too closely about her. On the walls there were religious pictures which, despite their sombre tones of dull brown and green and red, gave off glimmerings of light on glaring days when the blinds were drawn. In the entrance hall was a print of a Madonna which had power to lift Tansy's heart from any depth.

Her heart sank often these days but was restored quickly. It was a heart which reacted to small shocks but readjusted itself when her mind overcame or chose to ignore the cause of the shock. Mostly the latter. Her heart was a vulnerable organ, clearly the centre of her being, which, when it wasn't sinking or floating upward, felt as if it were being flicked by darts of joy or sorrow, sometimes both together, to her bewilderment.

First Year occupied the wide side verandah, wreathed with bougainvillea parted only at the steps where the glossy dark leaves formed an arch. Trails of blossom, crimson and purple, waved in the breeze, appearing to scrape against the deep blue sky. Beyond was the rose garden, a series of beds and arbours and little paths and rustic seats where the old nuns sat to take the morning sunshine. Those black clad figures appealed to Tansy. They sat so still; they looked so content.

The rose garden was orderly and pretty and scented. It seemed a pity that its continuation was the cabbage patch, but then, in their season, the cabbages waxed fat and crisply green and the hoses sprayed arches of rainbow water from all sides. The cabbage patch was bounded by the stout stone fence which shut off the convent from the rest of the world.

On the verandah one heard Sister Paul clattering her pots in the kitchen, ripplings and squee-awks and trillings from the music rooms, the drone of children at their lessons and Old Jack trundling his mower over the lawns.

Sister set their lessons and off she went to the prep room, the rec room, or back to the school. Her return was heralded by a patter of kid shoes, the swish and rattle of the rosary beads hanging from her girdle. They learnt to distinguish this sound above all others. But they learnt also that Sister could be unpleasantly stern if she felt they had idled during her absence. Unless they had a good excuse — perhaps Sister Paul had needed them to open the front door to visitors, or dust the banisters, or maybe they had swept the paths of the rose garden for Old Jack so that fallen leaves or dirt wouldn't blow on the old nuns — Sister was difficult to bring round. She became haughty and could remain that way for a week. When Sister's friendship was withdrawn they felt just awful.

Mostly they were good. Learning things for the fun of it was pleasant. They liked Sister to stay with them for a while when she came. She sat between them on the form and leant her head against the brick wall. Her eyes flicked over the rose garden, the old nuns, the cabbage patch and Old Jack and his mower as if she saw all that was there and more besides. She talked, not only of their lessons but about the convent outside Paris where she had spent her childhood, about the troubles of 1916 in Dublin, of a summer spent in Italy, of life in China. Sister had been everywhere and seen everything, it seemed.

She often descended on them with unusual requests. "I want you to write a story for the kindergarten class."

"What about, Sister?"

"You were five once, weren't you?" What sort of stories did you like then?"

"Hans Christian Andersen," said Janet.

"Grandfather told me stories and I liked them, but Mother didn't," said Tansy.

"There you are. Write one each. Perhaps you could leave out what your mother didn't like in your grandfather's stories, Tansy. It is for the kindergarten."

"Oh, things go over their heads," said Tansy.

"Did they ever go over yours?"

"No," admitted Tansy.

Meredith said Tansy got a lot from the convent. She called it education. Tansy didn't give any name to it, but whatever it was it satisfied her.

Meredith was not sorry they had given up the scholarship and allowed the government to keep the money. That sort of thing was all very well for people like the Rowlands who appeared to need money. What were a few shillings compared with a girl's happiness? She bent over the sewing machine and pedalled harder. She sang: "The saucy little bird in Nelly's hat" happily as she pedalled. Other people might know other songs, but a song had to enter her heart for her to know it. She knew only those she had learnt in her brief girlhood. She clung to them. No song had entered her heart since.

Meredith was pleased that, as Tansy grew older, she showed no inclination to join the rowdy element. There was a lamp post at the corner of the street where, at night, girls hung about with boys. From her own front steps Meredith watched them. She would call Tansy and ask, "Isn't that Jill Hogan? Why, she's younger than you. I wonder what her parents are thinking of!"

Tansy was non-committal. She was not interested in Jill Hogan or boys and girls under lamp posts. And she was certainly not interested if Meredith were looking for an opportunity to discuss matters arising from lamp-post gatherings.

Like most things in Tansy's life her lack of interest in the rough element was accidental. She had her own friends and was interested solely in them. There was Janet, with whom she spent her days at the convent. There was Dolores, now away at boarding school and strangely dim, seeing Tansy had known her so well for so long. She remembered Dolores' voice better than her face. It echoed in the occasional answer received in reply to a letter of her own.

Dear Tansy,

Thank you for your nice long letter about *The Scarlet Pimpernel*. It must be very enjoyable. I would like to read a lot, but at the moment just haven't the time. However, I look forward, when this is all over, to reading *The Scarlet Pimpernel*, and will tell you exactly what I think of it. After your vivid description I know I shall like it, too.

Ever,
Your true friend,
Dolores

There was Cassandra. Why she remembered Cassandra's face over the passage of years and forgot that of Dolores was one of time's mysteries. She remembered clearly the afternoon she had clambered up the rock and, as her head popped over the top, Cassandra's head popped up the other side. The Moneypennys had moved away from near Aunt Ruby's shortly after Tansy's visit. She had not heard of Cassandra since. These things made the friendship more valid. Otherwise, why remember? Cassandra was somewhere, an older Cassandra, knees covered, but the same at heart as Tansy was still. She was Tansy's friend now as then.

Once, of course, there had been Miriam. The least said about Miriam the better, but she could not be eradicated from Tansy's mind. She had seen her change from a fragile, pretty child, to a heavy, dark young woman. Even the curls had gone. Miriam's hair, oiled and sleek with a blue-black shine, was swept back from her forehead, and ears to make a large bun on the top of her head. In this was set a jewelled comb. The small gold earrings were gone, replaced by large ones. She wore a light blouse and dark skirt and no shoes and stockings. Her breasts hung heavy inside the blouse, her skirt was pulled above her knees as she squatted on the steps where she lived all day. That was Miriam. She was a bigger disgrace to Goombudgerie than the girl from the sawmill had been. Tansy no longer passed that way but she knew Miriam was there all right.

Now there was Gladdy Gladstone. Gladdy taught with Tansy at River Jordan, Cuthie having donated Tansy's services to remind Tansy that she was an Anglican and no part of the convent. At least on Sundays. In many ways Tansy liked Gladdy, who was older and fussed over her a great deal. But Gladdy wanted to be best friends with her and she couldn't have that.

"What did she say yesterday?" Janet would ask on Monday mornings.

"Oh, she was at it again and can't see why not."

"But it's impossible. You're best friends with me."

The bother with Gladdy was that she was putting forth those claims which were so important in the Trenworth family. Her mother and Meredith had been friends in girlhood.

"Let me see," said Meredith, when Tansy told her about Gladdy. "Her mother must have been Molly Spencer that was. Her family were on Sundown then. It's in the brigalow country about fifty miles from Land's End. In those days of good horses fifty miles didn't matter. We rode over, Grand-dad and I, a couple of times a year and stayed overnight. I think it was about cows. Mr Spencer had the nearest bull. Yes, Molly and I were quite good friends. Fancy me nearly forgetting her."

Meredith grew quite excited and next afternoon was able to lay before Tansy information she had received from Aunt Jessie, who prided herself on acquaintance with every living soul in Goombudgerie.

"Molly Spencer married a Harry Gladstone. So Mrs Gladstone would be the very Molly Spencer I used to visit as a girl. She has her quiverful, I believe."

Oh, the silly way mothers said things!

"She has seven children," said Tansy stolidly.

"Three upright boys and four girls who have never caused her any worry," supplied Meredith.

"Gladdy wouldn't cause anyone any worry," said Tansy.

"What is she like?"

"She has a gold bracelet above her elbow with her hanky stuck in it."

"What an odd way to describe anyone!"

"I don't think so. And she has adenoids. Well, she snuffles and Janet says it's adenoids. I don't like that about her very much. Otherwise she's all right."

"Has she her mother's hair?" demanded Meredith.

"I've never seen her mother," muttered Tansy.

"Molly had glossy dark curls to her waist. Four layers of them."

"Gladdy hasn't got that. She's mouse-coloured, parted in the middle, with a slide each side, low down, where it turns at the ends."

"Straight?"

"Quite straight."

Meredith sighed. "A pity. I suppose the boys have the curls. It's always the way."

As if it mattered!

Gladdy was a healthy looking girl whom Tansy would have thought of as fat only Gladdy said she wasn't. She was crazy on "little florals" this summer and had a new one each Sunday, thin stuffs patterned in blues and reds and golds over a stout white petticoat. She had beads to go with each dress, long strings knotted but still reaching below the waist. She wore silk stockings and high-heeled shoes and wide-brimmed hats.

Tansy would not have aspired to Gladdy except that Gladdy had sought her out and insisted on friendship. Then the family matter cropped up. After that Gladdy assumed she was Tansy's best friend. Tansy had to let her assume it; Gladdy over-rode all objections. Besides, it was only on Sundays.

Then Gladdy asked Tansy to come to tea at her place. "Mother likes me to have my girl friends to tea," she said. "I'm to have my boy to tea later. But of course I have to wait for Mr Right to come along for that."

Perhaps the thing that fascinated Tansy most about Gladdy was her conversation. And when she mentioned Mr Right, which she did frequently, she gave a sideways glance which conjured up unspeakable felicities.

"Gladdy wants me to go to tea at her place," Tansy reported to Meredith.

"Oh, how nice!" exclaimed Meredith. "You don't mix enough with boys and girls of your own age."

Tansy had the feeling that Meredith's mind was more on the three upright Gladstone boys than on Gladdy. Surely she wasn't thinking of a Mr Right for Tansy so soon? *She* who had picked a Mr Wrong?

Tansy giggled, thinking what a fine name this was for George. Next time Granny or Cuthie said "Someone-better-not-mentioned," she would answer, "I daresay you are referring to Mr Wrong". But then she would be told she was being cheeky. Grown-ups could say anything they wanted; if she thought of anything smart it was wiser left unsaid.

"What is it?" asked Meredith.

"Nothing," said Tansy.

"Nothing. Always nothing. Why won't you tell me things, Tansy?"

"I was. I was telling you about Gladdy. And I don't see the need to mix with a lot of boys and girls, Mother. I've got Janet, you know."

"Janet is a dear, sweet girl," said Meredith, "but when you're young it doesn't do to merge all your interest in one person. You need to expand."

"I like only people I like," replied Tansy, "and so do you, Mother."

"But I'm older. It's all very well when one is older. When I was your age —" Meredith sighed and considered. She put her head on one side and looked at Tansy, her eyes green and searching, bright and alive against the deepening sallowness of her skin. It was only in her eyes and dark, piled hair with its escaping tendrils that her girlhood beauty still showed. The hair was lovely but dreadfully old-fashioned. The style had lingered on in Goombudgerie and on chocolate boxes for some years.

But even painted girls on chocolate boxes were bobbed now. "I don't know whether times have changed," she continued, "or whether it's just my position, but I don't seem able to give you girls the things I had. Granny and Grand-dad are strait-laced as you know. Our life was simple, but we did have our pleasures. Picnics at the river, a dance in the woolshed to end the shearing. There was a dance every week or so in the season. Everyone went. Children danced from the time they could toddle. At your age, Tansy, I danced the clock round. I was quite a belle, you know," Meredith said eagerly.

Tansy looked as disapproving as she could. She did not like this sort of reminiscence.

But Meredith was well launched. "I never lacked for partners. There wasn't a boy in the district who didn't make it clear he wanted my favours."

There she went again. Favours, of all things!

"But surely you don't want me running around with boys?" asked Tansy. "How would you like it if you and Marny were on the steps and I was under the lamp post with those others?" Her mind continued when her voice had stopped: "Or if I were like Miriam?"

"That's what you don't understand," said Meredith, impatient at this childish interruption, when she wanted to impart a little of her own experience. "In the first flush of girlhood, contact with boys is happy and innocent. They are so shy and worshipping. Nothing but a glance, a touch on the hand —"

"Mother!" exclaimed Tansy.

"Every girl should have it. She's missing something if she doesn't," went on Meredith. She went on and on. Tansy had to stand there and hear it all. One of those talks which said too little and too much at the same time and which Tansy hated.

And all because Gladdy Gladstone had asked her to tea!

Tansy took some time deciding whether or not she would go to the Gladstones' to tea.

She sometimes stayed to tea with Cuthie, held formally in

the sitting room, Tansy pouring and Cuthie interrupting her gossip about the Rector to warn her to be careful of the thin cups which had been brought from England wrapped in Cuthie's woollen underwear, and which Tansy might own some day if Cuthie had a mind to let her have them, and if Tansy didn't break them in the meantime.

She sometimes stayed at Janet's, where they helped themselves from the tea table, piled what they wanted on plates and resorted to the hammock slung between the mulberry and the maple tree in Janet's back yard. There they ate with their fingers and talked without interruption from their elders.

Tea at the Gladstones' seemed different. Formidable, when one considered the three upright boys, the four girls who had never caused a moment's worry, and Mr and Mrs Gladstone.

Finally, prompted by Meredith, Tansy accepted.

Gladdy acknowledged her pleasure by squeezing Tansy hard. As Tansy's head came level with Gladdy's bust, which was all of one piece, an uplifted prominent roll, exuding a smell of talcum powder, she found Gladdy's embraces embarrassing. Gladdy was a girl of impulse who embraced often and at unexpected moments.

A Saturday was chosen for the event. Six-thirty the hour. This surprised Tansy. They had tea at four and called the next meal "supper". This was an evening affair. The whole evening, apparently. A date several weeks ahead was fixed. It appeared that the Gladstone household needed time to adjust itself to the most inauspicious visitor.

This gave Gladdy plenty of time to make oblique references to the occasion when others were present, to take Tansy aside and remind her that she was coming to tea on the fifteenth, tell her that everyone was thrilled about it. The Gladstones were just dying to meet Gladdy's friend. It also gave Meredith plenty of time to speculate about the three upright boys.

Tansy's wardrobe was not extensive at this time. The scraps donated by Meredith's customers were no longer any use even as trimming. Tansy had her own pride and refused to appear in

Goombudgerie trimmed in the remains of somebody's outfit, having in her younger days been taken for Mrs So-and-so's little girl when they both appeared at a church bazaar arrayed in green-and-white hailstone muslin. Cuthie gave a length of material now and again as a present, but no one else did, certainly not Granny Trenworth. Cuthie, being practical, gave the blue madapollam to make the convent dresses. These and the white voile, which had now graced several St Patrick night's concerts, were Tansy's sole dresses.

When Tansy wore the voile to church on the Sunday preceding Gladdy's teaparty, it was as usual. But when she put it on the next Saturday afternoon it had become short-waisted, the armholes tight, the already narrow hem perilously close to revealing her knees.

"You've grown out of it," said Meredith with the despair of one who knows there is no remedy. It would have to be worn. "And your legs look so long."

It wasn't her legs which had been dismaying Tansy, but she was pleased to divert her attention to them.

"Only stockings would cover them. I don't suppose the ones Aunt Ruby sent you last Christmas —"

"No; they went into holes."

"Yours always do," sighed Meredith. "You'll have to wear mine."

"Not the good silk, Mother!"

"They're all I've got. I was so foolish. I went to Chaselings' for two ordinary pairs and they were on the counter. I touched the lovely silk —"

Yes, Tansy knew. Meredith's dove grey, French silk stockings had sent the bill soaring.

"Give them to me," said Tansy grimly.

"You mustn't worry if anything happens to them. Stockings don't really matter."

Stockings don't matter. Sandals don't matter, only the exigency of living seems to matter. Very well. Tansy wouldn't give a damn!

"They make your legs look nice, dear. You have nice legs, long and slim. Like mine. I have nice legs. That's why I like nice stockings." Meredith gave a little laugh. "But then, women with most dreadful legs say they buy good stockings to make their legs look better. It's all awfully silly, isn't it?"

Yes; awfully, frightfully silly! Too silly to talk about!

"Women are queer, aren't they? The things they set store by. You see it in dressmaking. The oldest, most ill-favoured woman is vain, never too old to worry over a flabby bust or hamlike thighs. I wonder —"

Oh, dear! Tansy wasn't going to stand this. "Men are the same," she said firmly. "Janet's father is dieting to rid himself of his paunch."

"What! John with a paunch. I haven't noticed. He was so lean and tall, a veritable scarecrow as a youth."

Veritable indeed! If her mother would only stop reading those books from the School of Arts, she would not use such dreadful words. And she was smiling to herself as she always did when Doctor John was mentioned! Why the devil hadn't she married him and given Tansy a life like Janet's? Mummy and Daddy and Janet all so interested in one another and friendly, saying the most impossible things to each other in plain straight words. Janet unaware that one couldn't always have what one wanted and unmindful of exigencies. Tansy was pleased Janet had these things, but . . .

Tansy stared at herself in the oval mirror of the varnished pine wardrobe. The afternoon sunshine pouring through the crepe-curtained windows did nothing to hide any defects of frock, of face, of figure. Though the defects of figure were natural, Tansy disliked them above all else. Though her legs were straight and slim, in their coating of dove grey they looked surprising between the starched white dress and the black school sandals. Her arms came out of the sleeves of the dress and hung. Her white-skinned face was blotched at the sides of the nose and on the chin with pimples. Her mouth was pale and without shape. Her eyes were no colour at all, not blue, nor grey, nor Meredith's bright green. The hair she had thought well trained stood out in a brown shock from her head, waving one way then the other, rough curls robbing it of smoothness. Tansy had known she wasn't a beauty. She hadn't cared. But now she saw herself as an unutterable wretch and turned away from the mirror, disgusted.

"Tansy," said Meredith firmly, "you must not worry about those stockings. You look quite worked up."

"I'm not worried about the stockings."

"Well, what is the matter?"

"Nothing."

"Nothing again!" sighed Meredith. "I wish you wouldn't take your nothings so hard. Remember when you burnt your sandals — ?"

"I've remembered all that!" cried Tansy.

"There's no need to snap at me," reproved Meredith. "I can hardly say a thing these days." She was sitting on the edge of the bed, her spectacles held by the earpieces in one hand. She was blinking her eyes, as she had read that blinking relieved eyestrain. It made her look foolish, Tansy considered. The blinking was growing to be a habit when the glasses were off.

The bedroom, in the bright glare of the afternoon sunshine, appeared as wretched to Tansy as she felt she looked. There were the wardrobe, the dressing-table, the double bed with its honeycomb quilt, the washstand with its old-fashioned dish and ewer, the ledge beneath with the chamber which Meredith would keep there and which made Tansy nearly die when Janet came into the room.

"Oh, to get away from it all," went through her head, "and from her." She was so startled by the latter that she went to Meredith and flung her arms about her.

"I do hate to have to wear your stockings, Mother."

"That's all right, darling, as I told you." Meredith laid her cheek against what was to her the very smooth cheek of this girl of hers. She had a comforted, contented feeling at the contact.

Tansy allowed it for a moment then drew away. "I am rather silly, Mother. Do you know, I think I'm nervous."

"Well, if you're nervous about a simple thing like going to tea with a girl, what will you be like —"

"Oh, no!" Tansy broke in quickly. "Gladdy often looks a sight, too."

"You don't look a sight, dear. You look very nice. But we can pretty you up a little, I think." Meredith opened her hand to reveal a pair of earrings, tiny pearls forming a bunch of grapes, set on a gold leaf. HE had given them to Meredith when Tansy was born, Tansy knew; the way HER mind worked, she saw this as a fitting occasion for Tansy to wear them.

Tansy submitted while Meredith pushed the hair back behind her ears and placed the earrings on the lobes.

"Exquisite," said Meredith when she had done.

Tansy submitted also while Meredith dusted her face with the swansdown puff which was kept in the box of rice powder.

That was enough. Tansy kissed her hastily and escaped through the door.

"Say goodbye to Marny," Meredith called.

Tansy went to the back steps and waved to Marny, who was sitting with her friend Ruth Potter on the seat under the cedar tree. Both fair heads were bent over the one book. They did not look up. Tansy contemplated this picture of childish equanimity for a second, turned and fled through the house, jumped over the steps and ran to the gate.

"Tansy," Meredith's voice came to her as she banged the gate after her, "don't rush like that. It makes the face red and the hair dishevelled."

Tansy quickened her pace and disappeared around the corner in a cloud of dust.

A recently passed car had left the dust, but it seemed to Meredith that Tansy's flying heels had made it. The convent influence was wearing off, she thought. Before she had even left it!

* * *

Tansy arrived at Gladstone's in a state in which she had not been since babyhood. She was mute. This surprised herself more than the Gladstones, who thought she was shy. As the Gladstones were a family who thought girls should be shy it didn't matter.

She became more normal in Gladdy's bedroom, looking at the curtains, the treasures saved from childhood, the milk jug covers being made for the bazaar. But when they went into tea the same state returned. She didn't have a word to say for herself. Again it didn't matter. It was assumed in the Gladstone family that Mr Gladstone would do all the talking. He did.

After tea they washed and wiped up, everyone helping. As Tansy was wiping a little pink jug, Gladdy told her how valuable it was, hundreds of years old.

"Why do you use it?" asked Tansy.

"We never do. Only tonight for you."

The jug slipped out of Tansy's hand onto the floor and smashed into many pieces, just as Hetty Cooper's gravy boat and Aunt Bessie's jam jar had done, years ago.

There were cries of dismay, everyone bent to gather up the fragments of china and said there was certainly no hope of putting it together again.

"Don't worry, Tansy," said Mrs Gladstone. "It could have happened to any of us. It was only a jug anyway, whatever its worth. We'll forget it."

But the jug, its value and oldness kept cropping up. While Mrs Gladstone knew she should put the pieces in the rubbish tin, she didn't feel that she could. She put them on top of the china cabinet in the drawing room where, when they went into music, they faced Tansy all night.

Muriel, the second girl, played. Classical pieces with no words. Tansy took up as small a space as she could in one of the best chairs, tried to avoid looking at the pieces of jug or at anything else, and managed to stay at the end of each piece, "That was very nice."

However, she was shaken with a desire to giggle. She had to cough into her handkerchief and every now and again made a burbling sound, at which everyone looked at her.

She was relieved when at last Muriel rose from the piano and said, "I'm afraid that's the lot."

Tansy's hoped her final giggle sounded like a sigh of regret.

"We don't always have supper," said Mrs Gladstone, "but we're having it tonight for you, Tansy."

So they had supper. Walnut biscuits which Gladdy had made and cocoa. The Gladstones seemed to like it very much, though it was interrupted by the winding of clocks, the bolting of doors, and a discussion as to whether the large or small milk billy should be put on the gate for the milkman. Tansy felt her heart lightening. She knew that when supper was over she could go home. A vision of herself winging across the dark and silent town, alone and free, filled her with more animation than she had shown all night.

But it was not to be. The Gladstones had their own ideas about these things.

"As you have so far to go and it's very dark, Ronny will see you home," said Mrs Gladstone.

Tansy nearly shouted, *"What?"* Instead she said, "Oh no, Mrs Gladstone, I wouldn't put him to the bother. I take my great-grandmother home from church at night, then go home by myself."

"Ronny would not dream of letting a girl of your age cross town at night by herself," said Ronny's mother.

Tansy thought Ronny looked capable of doing just that. She thought he said, "Aw gee, Mum," but his words were drowned in voices saying goodnight and Gladdy assuring her that she would see her at River Jordan tomorrow.

Ronny was the eldest of the three boys, near her own age. He worked in the leather store, which he liked, for which he got fifteen shillings a week. His mother allowed him three shillings a week for himself. He told Tansy this as they walked along. They passed the saleyards, redolent with the smell of wool. They passed the railway station, now in darkness, only the rails gleaming in starlight, leading away to cattle and sheep runs west, cities east.

So far it wasn't too bad. Ronny was well over on his side of the footpath, she on hers.

But when they came to the narrow railway bridge they bumped together in attempting to ascend the steps at the same time. Ronny put his hand on Tansy's elbow to steady her and kept it there while they crossed the bridge. Ronny's hand was hot and Tansy didn't feel comfortable about it but didn't like to move her elbow in case Ronny thought that she thought he was doing it intentionally instead of for politeness. They were both breathing heavily by the end of the bridge. Down the steps Ronny grasped her elbow tighter. She felt his breath against her ear and a kiss landed on her cheek.

She jerked her elbow away and stalked ahead.

"Aw gee," said Ronny, stumbling after her in the darkness. He caught up with her but walked apart.

When she could trust her voice Tansy said, "You can go home now."

"No. Mum said to see you home."

"Do you always kiss girls when your mother tells you to see them home?" asked Tansy.

"Yes," answered Ronny. "If they want to. But if you don't want to, I won't. There's not much in it anyway. Some girls like it, but. Girls like it better than fellows."

Tansy made a disbelieving sound. They walked on in silence. The far stars above Goombudgerie wheeled above their heads. She forgot Ronny. She forgot Gladdy. She forgot she had been to tea at the Gladstones'. She forgot Meredith would be waiting, propped on her pillows, her hair in plaits on her shoulders, her book held close to her eyes, to hear all about it.

Tansy forgot everything but her surprise at finding that she liked boys.

16 A great girl must come to the end of her schooldays. When Janet left the convent to go to boarding school, Tansy lingered on a while clinging to it as a place she knew, where she fitted in and was happy. But she missed Janet and convent days grew dull without her. Besides, Tansy's conscience began to prick her. The machine whirring late into the night, Meredith's red-rimmed eyes in the morning, Marny passing the high school exam and insisting on attending the State high school despite the expense of books and uniform, Mr Chaselings' bill in arrears and Meredith not appearing to worry about it any more . . . all these things worried her.

She came home one afternoon and said she had left school.

"What!"

"Yes, Mother. I've learnt all Sister can teach me."

"What did Sister say?" asked Meredith.

"Nothing," replied Tansy, which was true. As it had only occurred to Tansy on the way home to leave, there was nothing Sister could say. Tansy, like Cuthie, did things when she thought of them.

Now Tansy and Meredith had their days together. The first real companionship of her life, Meredith said, and was happy in it. But Tansy found it dull. Time hung heavily. She was thrown back suddenly with Meredith, Cuthie and Aunt Jessie and no longer found their excitements hers. Because she had gone to the convent she had grown apart from the girls with whom she would have normally grown up. Janet was home only one weekend a month. Mr Right had appeared for Gladdy and she was now engrossed in being best friends with him. It perplexed Tansy that life could flatten out so, just as it had appeared to be merging into something.

But someday something would happen. It must.

At first Meredith had the idea of doing something with Tansy. There was sewing. If she taught Tansy to sew, she could help her and between them they might do very well. But it turned out that as far as sewing was concerned, Tansy did not have the gift. Meredith believed in the gift. She knew that without it, trying to do anything was useless. Also, Meredith as a teacher was impatient. She no sooner set Tansy a task than she took it from her. "Here, I'll do that. What a way to go about it!"

There were jobs which girls could do these days. Or there had been. Just at the time when Tansy needed one, they disappeared suddenly for a reason which neither Tansy nor Meredith understood clearly. There was a worldwide Depression. Their participation in it gave them the feeling of belonging somewhere, though Meredith, having known depression in many forms since her marriage, couldn't see why everyone was so startled about it or why it filled the papers with headlines.

However, when Cuthie told them that Tottie Sparrow was leaving her job at the Western Stores to be married, and Tansy went to see about it and came home disheartened, Meredith was able to tell her that a man on Wall Street, New York, had shot himself because he had no position either.

Tottie's job had been dusting china and the pay was twelve and sixpence a week. While Tansy hadn't wanted to dust china, stared at all day by idling customers, she had perceived that the money would cover a number of exigencies. She felt that shooting oneself on Wall Street, New York, would be more exciting than being snubbed by the perky manager of the Western Stores, Goombudgerie. She didn't try any more. They let the Depression have its way and went on with their own life.

So it came about that Tansy kept house for Meredith and found pleasure in being rather good at it. Better than Meredith. Granny's lessons at Land's End, Cuthie's pernicketiness about her household affairs, had sunk in. Why they hadn't ever sunk into Meredith was a puzzle. The gift again, no doubt.

She went on messages also, as she had always done. But she went without pleasure. Goombudgerie, sweltering under its iron roofs in summer sun, swept by westerly winds in winter, afforded nothing new. She could have gone blindfolded.

Something must happen.

It did. Cuthie came over waving a letter. It happened to be Tansy's seventeenth birthday, but Cuthie forgot birthdays these days. She forgot much but still remembered a great deal.

The amaryllis was out full, a deep red bell on its pale green stem. The cedars were in bloom, a haze of mauve above the iron roofs of the houses. Away to the east the line of hills stood clear and blue. It was a day of such clear sunlight that you could see the whole town and the perspectives beyond. A house was only a shell around you.

Meredith had been vaguely and troublingly sentimental all morning. She stirred on Tansy's birthday as she never did on Marny's. She had no money for a present but had tried to put into words the things she would have given Tansy if she could. Both she and Tansy were conscious that Tansy was now the same age as she had been when she ran away with George. Tansy knew that Meredith wanted to tell her about it, but she felt there were limits on a birthday and gave no opportunity.

Ten years ago Cuthie had admitted to being old. She did not do so now. Once she had been prepared to wait cheerfully for death, but she was an impatient woman and its tardiness caused her to give up the whole idea. She was thinner, her white skin criss-crossed with lines; but her back was straight, her voice brisk. She waved the letter at Meredith.

"Ruby Buckland, no less. She's bought that house at last. What poor Tom left matured and — here, read it for yourself. Such a rigmarole. Ruby all over."

"Ruby's writing has grown more difficult," said Meredith, blinking her eyes, then adjusting her glasses.

"She says you'll know where the house is, Tansy," went on Cuthie. "It's near the pipe where Barcroft Boake hanged himself."

"We couldn't find the pipe, Cuthie," said Tansy. "Remember?"

"No, I don't. But I daresay it doesn't hurt to forget a few

things. We all do," said Cuthie sturdily. "She moved the bougainvillea from the old house to the new one, but it hasn't struck. She wants another one. And she also wants the pink ivy geranium which I brought from her mother's place on Derrick Plains to my place by the river —"

"How are you going to send them down?" asked Meredith, giving up the attempt to read Ruby Buckland's writing and taking off her glasses.

"Send them? Why, I'll take them! She's asked me to come and stay."

"But Cuthie, you're —"

"I'm what?" demanded Cuthie.

Meredith looked helplessly at Tansy. Tansy avoided her eyes.

Something had happened.

When Cuthie went, she went. A week later, in the early hours of a summer morning, Tansy sat beside her in the train pulling out from Goombudgerie station. The rails led west to the cattle and sheep runs; they led east to the cities. Tansy was going east.

She was going with Cuthie to Aunt Ruby Buckland in Sydney for a holiday as she had done once before. Meredith and Marny, when school broke up, were going to Land's End as they had done before. Life repeated itself. It was the same. Only in her heart Tansy knew it wasn't the same.

The train stopped outside the town to take on water. It stopped a little later to let a pig train pass.

Soon, behind lay her own town, with Meredith and Marny alone in the small house on Palm-grove Street. Behind lay Land's End, where the walls still whispered old stories to those who wished to hear. Behind lay Granny and Grand-dad and the Sawpit Tree. Behind lay Grandfather, sleeping peacefully in the grave from which you could see the blue line of hills, and over which blew the free wind from the plain. Behind lay her childhood.

The train went on. The sun came up. The trees curtsied by

on the golden and black plains. The train would go on and on. Tonight she would be in another train across the Queensland border.

"They scattered to the four corners of the state, but they didn't cross the MacIntyre," she said aloud.

"What was that?" asked Cuthie.

Tansy smiled at her but did not answer. She was escaping. She was free.

From now on she would cross any border she wanted to cross.

UQP YOUNG ADULT FICTION

The Great Secondhand Supper   *Greg Bastian*

Acting on inside information about a proposed link road, Jason Washington and his family leave the city to open a restaurant in Gum Flats. When the road fails to appear, the Washingtons are threatened with disaster. Jason plans to save the day by writing a prize-winning story, "The Great Secondhand Supper", and shares his ambition with Angela Conti, his vivacious schoolmate.

Merryll of the Stones   *Brian Caswell*

A splendid story of time travel and magic which begins in Sydney, when Megan discovers she is the sole survivor of a motor accident. She awakes strangely haunted by dreamlike memories. When she goes to live in Wales, these lead her into a mystic ancient world. **Honour book — Children's Book of the Year (1990) and Children's Book Award, Adelaide Festival Awards for Literature (1990).**

The Heroic Life of Al Capsella   *Judith Clarke*

Nothing is more important to fourteen-year-old Al Capsella and his friends than being "normal". Yet despite his heroic efforts to conform, Al faces a crippling pair of obstacles: his mother and father. **Shortlisted — NSW Premier's Literary Awards (1989).**

Al Capsella and the Watchdogs   *Judith Clarke*

Brilliant sequel to *The Heroic Life of Al Capsella*. Al and his friends can see the end of their schooldays approaching — life is changing and it's a bit scary. The "Watchdogs" are the anxious mothers of these suburban teenagers; and in spite of his own Watchdog, Mrs Capsella, Al manages to fall into some hilarious situations.

The Boy on the Lake   *Judith Clarke*
Stories of the Supernatural

In this spinechilling collection of weird and spooky stories, nothing is as it first appears. Judith Clarke's unpredictable imagination creates a very human world — charged with the power of mystery and the supernatural.

The Boys from Bondi   *Alan Collins*

The world of young Jacob and Solly Kaiser falls apart when they are orphaned and pitched into a Sydney children's home which is filled with refugee Jewish children from Hitler's Europe. **Shortlisted — USA National Jewish Book Award (1989).**

The Inheritors *Jill Dobson*

Twenty-five years after a nuclear war, a community of survivors live on beneath a protective dome. Sixteen-year-old Claudia, a promising youth leader, begins to question her society's oppressive values and wonder about life outside the dome's security.

Time to Go *Jill Dobson*

In this powerful second novel by the young author of *The Inheritors*, two artistic teenage girls are determined to escape their stifling country lives. A brilliant and moving counterpoint is formed as Laura Phillips, dedicated flautist, and Danny Bird, aspiring dancer, explore the themes of creativity and love.

Summer Press *Rosemary Dobson*

Twelve-year-old Angela Read is left to her own devices one summer in the ancient village of Hadlow, England. She knows no one — until she meets the forthright Lily, the mysterious and tragic Sarah, and a scary silent boy.

Lonely Summers *Nora Dugon*

Nora Dugon's appealing first novel is the story of a teenage survivor, Kelly Ryan, who befriends an impulsive elderly woman. Together this unlikely pair face excitement and danger in an inner city neighbourhood.

Clare Street *Nora Dugon*

A sequel to *Lonely Summers:* Kelly Ryan's seventeenth year brings her first experience of love and her first taste of a settled existence within her innercity neighbourhood.

A Season of Grannies *James Grieve*

Of all the hare-brained schemes that Jacqui Barclay is involved with, the Rent-a-Granny enterprise is perhaps the craziest. And it leads to others, including a very peculiar relationship with Looch, the Spaghetti Eater. **Shortlisted — Guardian (UK) Children's Book of the Year Award (1988).**

Sooner or Later *Sophie Masson*

Scilla comes to Hogan's Creek to live for a while with her grandmother, Rosie, who is dying. During those few months, Scilla slowly learns to accept the inevitability of Rosie's death. She reaches, too, a new understanding with her estranged father, and discovers the beginning of romance with Vernon, a fellow pupil at the local school.

McKenzie's Boots   *Michael Noonan*

Six feet four and only 15 years old, McKenzie and his boots went to fight the Japanese in New Guinea, finding adventure, courage and a true humanity beyond wartime propaganda. *McKenzie's Boots* was chosen for the 1988 list of Best Books for Young Adults by the Young Adult Services division of the American Library Association.

The Patchwork Hero   *Michael Noonan*

Young Hardy is the narrator of this story, set in a coastal township during the Depression of the 1930s. Hardy's mother has died; his father, Barney, is a happy-go-lucky tugboat captain — his "Patchwork Hero". One fine day Marie enters their lives — and from that moment everything changes. A new edition of this classic story of childhood, which has been successfully adapted for television.

The December Boys   *Michael Noonan*

Choker, Spark, Maps, Fido and Misty: these are the "December Boys", so-called because they are all thought to have been born in that month. From an outback orphanage they come to a seaside inlet for the Christmas holidays and see the ocean for the first time . . . and the beautiful, cartwheeling Teresa. A new edition of this well-loved classic of Australian childhood.

The Other Side of the Family   *Maureen Pople*

Katharine Tucker, fifteen, is sent from England to her grandparents in Sydney to escape wartime bombing. Once there, she's sent to the bush, to the strange township and eccentric home of her legendary Grandma Tucker. Maureen Pople's first novel for teenagers has been selected as a School Library Jounral USA Best Book of the Year (1988), and nominated for the South Carolina Young Adult Book of the Year Award (1990-1991).

Pelican Creek   *Maureen Pople*

Two teenage girls, living a century apart, are drawn together by a secret in Maureen Pople's absorbing new novel for young adults. Living with friends in rural New South Wales while her parents' marriage breaks up, Sally Matthews finds a mysterious relic from the area's romantic past.

The Road to Summering   *Maureen Pople*

Rachel Huntley's formerly peaceful family life seems to be breaking up all around her. Her father's new partner, Caroline, and the disappearance of her brother, young George, are somehow bound up with the secret of the old house called "Summering".

Rookwood   Dorothy Porter

"Tom": that's what Jackie's grandmother always calls her. At fourteen, Jackie doesn't like it (she doesn't like her grandmother, either). It's only after Jackie embarks on a school project, "Your Family Tree", that Jackie discovers the hidden events in her grandmother's life that explain a great deal. Finally, she decides it's time the secrets were brought into the open . . .

Long White Cloud   *James G. Porter*

The Long White Cloud that guided the ancient Maoris to their new land is not the only cloud hanging over Gil Cook's head. His family has moved to New Zealand, to live on a small farm. When Gil leaves home intent on returning to Australia, he meets with more difficulties than he bargained for.

The Edge of the Rainforest   *James G. Porter*

Karen Emerson and her mother live in a small farming community in the beautiful Atherton Tablelands rainforest. When their lifestyle is threatened by a conservative neighbour, family tensions run high, and an engrossing quest for identity begins for Karen.

The Sky Between the Trees   *James Preston*

Not a book about superheroes, just a farm boy who fulfilled his ambition to become one of Australia's great axe-men. This is the stuff that Australian myths are made of.

Flight of the Albatross   *Deborah Savage*

Teenager Sarah Steinway leaves her New York home to visit her scientist mother on Great Kauri Island, New Zealand. Sarah's rescue of an injured albatross and her meeting with Mako, a Maori boy her own age, are the linked events which make her stay on the island the most memorable experience in her young life.

Blue Days   *Donna Sharp*

Marie Lucas has more than her share of the blues: her father has just died; her mother is in shock; her friends are disappointing and her boyfriend . . . Teenage life is complicated but Marie takes control at last. **Shortlisted — Children's Book of the Year (1987).**